PU
THE RI

Corruption is rife in the Aleph Cygni system and the flow of the illicit narcotic Satophil-d from the spaceports of the planet Kether has grown to enormous proportions. Several attempts have been made to crack the notorious drug rings of Kether, with no success. Now the hard-pressed Galactic Federation has entrusted YOU with this extremely dangerous undercover mission. YOU must find the source of the drug and bring all those concerned to justice. But beware! Kether is a wild and lawless place – and YOU are on your own. . .

Two dice, a pencil and an eraser are all you need to embark on this thrilling futuristic adventure, complete with its elaborate combat system and a score sheet to record your gains and losses.

Many dangers lie ahead and your success is by no means certain. Powerful adversaries are ranged against you and often your only choice is to kill or be killed!

Steve Jackson and Ian Livingstone present:

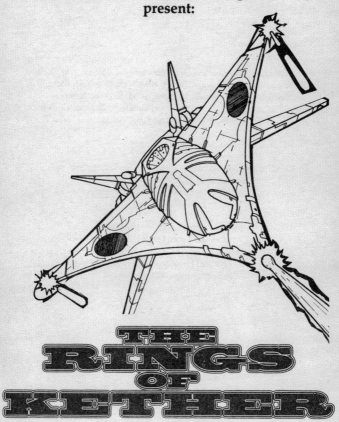

THE RINGS OF KETHER

Andrew Chapman

Illustrated by Nik Spender

Puffin Books

Puffin Books, Penguin Books Ltd, Harmondsworth, Middlesex, England
Viking Penguin Inc., 40 West 23rd Street, New York, New York 10010, U.S.A.
Penguin Books Australia Ltd, Ringwood, Victoria, Australia
Penguin Books Canada Ltd, 2801 John Street, Markham, Ontario, Canada L3R 1B4
Penguin Books (N.Z.) Ltd, 182–190 Wairau Road, Auckland 10, New Zealand

First published 1985

Concept copyright © Steve Jackson and Ian Livingstone, 1985
Text copyright © Andrew Chapman, 1985
Illustrations copyright © Nik Spender, 1985
All rights reserved

Made and printed in Great Britain by
Cox & Wyman Ltd, Reading
Filmset in 11/13pt Linotron Palatino by
Rowland Phototypesetting Ltd,
Bury St Edmunds, Suffolk

Except in the United States of America,
this book is sold subject to the condition
that it shall not, by way of trade or otherwise,
be lent, re-sold, hired out, or otherwise circulated
without the publisher's prior consent in any form of
binding or cover other than that in which it is
published and without a similar condition
including this condition being imposed
on the subsequent purchaser

CONTENTS

YOUR MISSION
7

ADVENTURE SHEET
14

MISSION BRIEFING
16

THE RINGS OF KETHER
19

YOUR MISSION

You are a Narcotics Investigator for the Galactic Federation. Recognized by your superiors as being among the best in the field, you have been issued with the latest in interstellar scout craft and dispatched, single-handed, to crack a suspected drug ring in the Aleph Cygni star system.

Before you can begin, though, you must determine your strengths and weaknesses. For this you will require two dice and a pencil to record scores on the *Adventure Sheet* on pages 14–15. As it is possible you will not successfully complete your mission in your first adventure, you may wish to take photocopies of the *Adventure Sheet* for future adventures.

Your Ship

Roll one die. Add 6 to the result. Enter this total under the WEAPONS STRENGTH section of the *Adventure Sheet*. When firing at enemy spacecraft, you will need to roll *less than* this to score a hit.

Roll one die. Enter this score in the SHIELDS section of your *Adventure Sheet*. You will lose points from this SHIELDS score whenever you are hit by fire from enemy spacecraft. If your ship is hit when your SHIELDS score is zero, your ship is destroyed.

Your Abilities

Your abilities to fight, withstand damage and escape from tricky situations are determined by your SKILL, STAMINA and LUCK. On your *Adventure Sheet* you will see sections where these attributes are to be recorded.

Roll one die. Add 6 to the result. Enter this total as your SKILL score.

Roll two dice. Add 12 to the result. Enter this total as your STAMINA score. If your STAMINA score ever reaches zero, you have been killed.

Roll one die. Add 6 to the result. Enter this total as your LUCK score.

Testing Your Luck

On occasion you will be called upon to *Test your Luck*. When this occurs, roll two dice. If the result *equals or is less than* your LUCK, you are successful. If the result *exceeds* your LUCK, you are unsuccessful. Each time you *Test your Luck*, reduce your LUCK score by 1 point.

Blaster Combat

Modern weapons being what they are, blaster combat is fairly short and extremely deadly. It is conducted as follows:

1. Roll two dice. If the result is *higher than or equal to* your SKILL, you have missed. If the result is *less than* your SKILL, you have hit your foe and inflicted damage on it – deduct 4 points from your opponent's STAMINA.
2. If your opponent's STAMINA has reached zero then your opponent has died.
3. If your opponent is still alive, then your fire will be returned: roll two dice. If the result is *higher than or equal to* your opponent's SKILL, your opponent has missed. If the result is *less than* your opponent's SKILL, your opponent has hit you – deducting 4 points from *your* STAMINA.
4. If you have not been killed, start a new combat round by returning to step 1.

Note: If you are faced by more than one opponent, you may select which one you will direct fire against. They will *all* return fire simultaneously (unless dead, of course).

Hand-to-hand Combat

Hand-to-hand combat is conducted just as in other Fighting Fantasy books. If you are already familiar with this system you can skip this part of the rules. Otherwise:

1. Combat is simultaneous. Hand-to-hand fighting is a series of clashes in which one combatant will do damage to the other.
2. Roll two dice. Add your opponent's SKILL score to the roll. The total is your opponent's Attack Strength.

3. Roll two dice again. Add your SKILL score to the roll. The total is your Attack Strength.
4. If your opponent's Attack Strength is higher than yours, the opponent has inflicted damage on you – deduct 2 points from your STAMINA.
5. If your Attack Strength is higher than your opponent's, you have inflicted damage on your opponent – deduct 2 points from your opponent's STAMINA.
6. If the Attack Strengths are equal, both attacks have missed. Start the next Attack Round from Step 2 above.
7. Continue this combat until either your STAMINA or your opponent's is reduced to zero (death).

Ship-to-ship Combat

There are two modes of attack in ship-to-ship combat:

1. *Phasers:* Whenever a ship is hit by phasers it will lose 1 point from its SHIELDS.
2. *Smart Missiles:* Only your ship is equipped with this weapon. When you decide to fire a Smart Missile at an enemy ship, the missile will automatically home in on and destroy the enemy ship, regardless of how many SHIELDS the enemy may have left.

Combat is conducted as follows:

1. You select your target(s). You may attack with both phasers and Smart Missiles in the same combat round, firing phasers at one ship while destroying another ship with a Smart Missile.
2. Any enemy vessels attacked by a Smart Missile are now destroyed; they will not return fire with phasers.
3. Roll two dice for the phaser attack. If the result is *higher than or equal to* your ship's WEAPONS STRENGTH, you have missed. Proceed to step 5.
4. If the result is *less than* your ship's WEAPONS STRENGTH, you have hit the enemy ship – reduce its SHIELDS by 1 point. If the enemy ship has not been destroyed, proceed to step 5.
5. All undestroyed enemy ships return fire with phasers in the following manner: roll two dice. If the result is *higher than or equal to* the ship's WEAPONS STRENGTH, the phasers have missed you.
6. If the result is *less than* the ship's WEAPONS STRENGTH, the phasers have hit you – reduce your SHIELDS by 1 point.
7. Combat continues from step 1 until either you or your opponent's ships are destroyed.

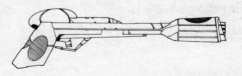

Smart Missiles

These deadly devices inflict instant and certain destruction upon enemy spacecraft. They can only be used once each. Your spacecraft begins with two of these weapons – note that there is a section on the *Adventure Sheet* for keeping record of the number of Smart Missiles you have left in your Armoury.

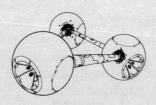

Replacing Stamina

If you become involved in any gun battles or other combat, you will almost certainly lose some STAMINA points. These may be recovered by taking Pep Pills. Each pill will restore 6 points to your STAMINA and can be taken at any time. You begin the adventure with 4 Pep Pills – note that there is a section on the *Adventure Sheet* for keeping record of the number of Pep Pills you have left. Your STAMINA score can never be made to exceed your *Initial* level.

Your Credit Account

During the course of your adventure you will probably need certain amounts of cash. You begin the mission with 5,000 kopecks (the standard intergalactic currency) – record this amount and any expenses on the *Adventure Sheet*.

ADVENTURE SHEET

SKILL
Initial 12
Skill= 12

STAMINA
Initial 20
Stamina= 24

LUCK
Initial 12
Luck= 11

12

EQUIPMENT AND WEAPONS

blaster
rifle
tube
compontents
key
sapholited

SHIELDS
Initial 4
Shields= 4

SMART MISSILES
2

PEP PILLS
4 4

MONEY
5760
5000
£3500

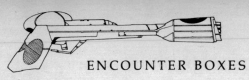

ENCOUNTER BOXES

Skill= Stamina=	Skill= Stamina=	Skill= Stamina=
Skill= Stamina=	Skill= Stamina=	Skill= Stamina=
Skill= Stamina=	Skill= Stamina=	Skill= Stamina=
Skill= Stamina=	Skill= Stamina=	Skill= Stamina=

MISSION BRIEFING

The Galactic Federation consists of several hundred civilized worlds, all of which are signatories to certain basic Federal laws and conventions. One of these concerns the suppression of trafficking in certain narcotic drugs. Simply, the export of narcotic drugs from one world to another is illegal.

The Federal Police Force has become aware, however, of an extremely large flow of the illicit narcotic Satophil-d from the tiny Aleph Cygni system. As the individual worlds are supposed to police these matters themselves, there has developed some concern that all is not well with the Aleph Cygni administration.

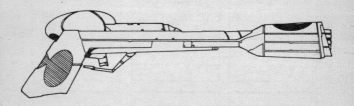

With the obvious failure of the local administration to deal with this breach of Federal law your department, Federal Central (Vice), has decided to send a Grade 1 Investigator (you) to locate the source of this drug flow, penetrate the organization responsible and then destroy it.

Because of the possible untrustworthiness of the Aleph Cygni authorities, you travel to the system incognito, posing as an interstellar travelling salesman with a cargo of exotic off-world fruit, spices and luxuries. Once in the system you are on your own. Good luck!

NOW TURN OVER.

1

FIVE MINUTES TO HYPERSPACE TERMINATION flashes on the command vidi in front of you. An alarm bell chimes softly through the ship. In a few moments you will be entering the Aleph Cygni system and, if there has been any criminal infiltration into the Galactic Vice Squad, there could be a very hot reception.

FOUR MINUTES TO HYPERSPACE TERMINATION

Swivelling in your crash couch, you run a check through your spacecraft's weapon systems: PHASERS – Check; SMART MISSILES, 2 – Check; SHIELDS – Check. Pretty hefty stuff for a travelling salesman, though no one's to know, unless you have to use it. Until such time, your cover should remain intact.

You charge up the conventional drive of your spaceship, raise the anti-spy beam shield and grit your teeth for the stomach twisting end to hyperspatial travel.

PREPARE FOR INSERTION INTO REAL SPACE/TIME

The bottom drops out of the spaceship; you follow at some super-light speed . . . *Ssshhh*. Everything flies back together and is once again, apart from the hangover you seem to have developed in the last moment, back to normal. There, on the screen in front of you, is the Aleph Cygni system – the yellow star, Aleph Cygni, and its single planet, Kether. Kether, your Cosmo-Nav tells you, is a habitable world consisting of vast expanses of ocean and, apart from a few scattered islands, only one continental land-mass. Circling this world is a small pock-marked moon known locally as Rispin's End. Not visible on your vidiscreen, but whose presence you are alerted to by your Cosmo-Nav, is a vast belt consisting of hundreds of thousands of asteroids.

Where will you begin your search for the drug runners – at the system's starport on Kether (turn to **333**), on the moon (turn to **328**), or in the asteroid belt (turn to **372**)?

2

He spots you following and ducks down a sidestreet. You try to give chase but he is nowhere to be seen. Lost him. Suddenly, a hand grabs your arm and drags you into the shadowy shelter between two buildings. It is the man you were chasing. 'Wha . . .?' you try to say before he claps a hand over your mouth. He pulls out a pad, scrawls *'Quiet – spy beam!'* on it and then *'Meet me, Hotel Mirimar – Rm 1201, 1 hour.'* Then he strides off.

Will you go to meet him (turn to **395**), or go back and continue your surveillance of Zera Gross's apartment (turn to **109**)?

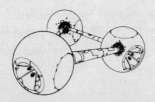

3

The door opens into a small room, with a desk, a few filing cabinets and a vidiphone. The vidiphone begins to buzz and, to your dismay, footsteps can be heard approaching. Drawing your blaster, you hide in a corner, behind a filing cabinet. Someone enters the room and answers the phone.

'Yeah? Oh, it's you, baby,' says a man.

'Clive, I have to see you,' a woman's voice crackles over the phone.

'Look, dear, we're going to be busy all night *and* I have to meet Arthur at the Café Heroes of the Federation tomorrow morning, so you'll have to wait until after then.'

'But . . .' she pleads.

'Tomorrow. We can't speak here.' He hangs up.

'*Hey*, Torus? Get here, now!' yells someone elsewhere in the building.

'OK!' Clive yells back, running from the room.

Will you leave and go to the meeting that Clive is having with Arthur tomorrow (turn to **315**), or will you continue to explore the warehouse (turn to **354**)?

4

In a sleazy bar you discover a hoary old asteroid miner, down from space for a two-week drinking-binge. 'Lots of illicit traffic . . . hee hee,' he cackles. 'Lots of illicit traffic, my little Fed . . . hee, hee . . . but it'll cost you 500 kopecks to get the location out of me.'

Will you pay him the 500 kopecks (turn to **355**), or go to the starport to continue your inquiries (turn to **345**)?

5

'Stop!' you cry, 'leave me alone!' It shrieks with insane laughter, rises to its full height, pounces – and swallows you whole. You have failed.

6

You show him your identification. 'You . . . you're a Fed?' he asks. 'I . . . I didn't mean . . . Oh, no!' His bewilderment gives way to fear. 'I didn't do any-thing,' he says, putting his blaster down. 'I'm not like the rest of the guys here . . . I don't work for *them*.'

'Who?' you ask, but he is not listening. In a panic, he runs off, and disappears from view. Will you go back into hiding again (turn to **357**), or assume that your cover has been blown and leave the starport in search of a new lead (turn to **231**)?

7

The road dips into a hollow, thus being forced into an S-bend. The sloop, still far ahead, slowed down and stayed on the road to take this bend. Will you do the same (turn to **280**), or throw the car into the possibly soft shoulder at high speed (turn to **358**)?

8

You hit them a glancing blow, but enough to send them spinning across the tarmac. When the sloop hits the verge it flips, end over end, until it comes to rest in a tree a few metres back from the road. You pull over. Turn to **359**.

9

The corridor ends fairly shortly in a large control panel. The only thing on it which makes any sense is a digital read-out:

NEXT SHUTTLE DUE – 75 HOURS, 31 MINUTES, 20 SECONDS

You turn back to the T-junction and follow the other passage. Turn to **360**.

10

You go off target, drifting straight into the side of one of the bulbous creatures. The thing turns wild, sprouting teeth in a cavernous maw and snapping at you. It bites you. Lose 4 points of STAMINA. Turn to **361**.

11

Arriving at the Viqueque that evening, you find Mr Samuel, heavily disguised by a change of hair colour and false beard, seated in a semi-enclosed booth. 'Were you followed?' he whispers. 'I don't think so,' you whisper back. He relaxes, wiping his brow with an old handkerchief and taking a hearty slug from his drink. During dinner, via staccato bursts of whispers, he informs you that the local proctors are absolutely rotten with corruption and that his own department, the Vice Squad, is the worst.

'We haven't conducted any form of drug-related inquiry for months,' he laments. 'Somebody upstairs, perhaps everybody, is on someone's payroll.' He doesn't have many ideas, though, about who is controlling the racket, nor where you should begin. He has only two concrete leads to offer you. He suspects that some of the drugs arrive at the city's heliport on both legal and illegal flights, and he has one underworld contact – an unemployed starship navigator – who would be willing to speak with you.

Will you ask a few questions at the heliport (turn to **206**), or go to meet the navigator (turn to **284**)?

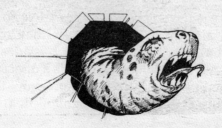

12

You punch the heading YEARBOOKS into the terminal. After a second it replies with

AGRICULTURE, MANUFACTURE OR TRANSPORT?

Which heading will you look up first?

Agriculture?	Turn to 363
Manufacturing?	Turn to 324
Transport?	Turn to 285

13

The gunman has collapsed on the sidewalk; a pool of blood is spreading towards the gutter. You approach him cautiously. He opens his eyes and watches you. 'Zera has you marked,' he whispers. 'We . . . took Clive to "Spark's" this . . . this morning . . . you're next.' He expires.

Looks like you won't be able to find Clive now – he's probably already six foot under. If 'they' are planning to drag you into a place called 'Spark's' (a bar, you discover, when looking it up in a directory a bit later), then perhaps you should pre-empt them by showing up at this place – incognito – first. Turn to 286.

14

You discover an alarm which would have been triggered had you simply opened the window. You easily disarm it. Climbing through the window you find yourself in a tiny bare room. Turn to 365.

15

Test your Luck. If you are successful, turn to 327; otherwise turn to 366.

16

You have no leads left to follow. Still, you persist for a few more weeks before receiving a recall from Federal Central (Vice). You have failed.

17

The track winds through the wood for a kilometre or two before breaking out into the open. You cannot see the sloop anywhere. Will you continue down this road (turn to 95), or backtrack to the main road (turn to 368)?

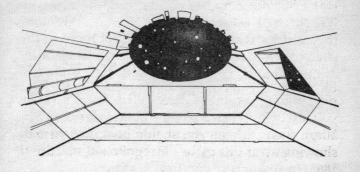

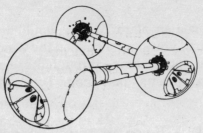

18

You duck to the side, avoiding his blow. Next, you deliver a savage kick to his midriff, knocking him to the floor. Throwing him into a full nelson, you demand, 'What's going on here?' He gurgles a bit and then tries pointing at his desk, on which are numerous files and a computer vidilink. You take a look at these. Turn to **125**.

19

You gently nudge your ship between the closely packed mines. Roll two dice. If the result is higher than or equal to your SKILL, turn to **351**. If the result is less than your SKILL, turn to **370**.

20

The corridor takes you to the control room of the asteroid's nuclear reactor. There are plenty of instrument panels covering the walls but, strangely, other than a keyhole, no controls – must be completely automatic.

If you have the key to fit this hole turn to **391**; otherwise you return to the T-junction and head down the other corridor (turn to **352**).

21

The corridor twists, turns and branches. Eventually you realize that you must have made a wrong turn somewhere, for the assassin is nowhere to be seen. You decide that you might as well follow him up on Kether, as he's unlikely to stay on Rispin's End once you leave. You rocket back to the planet and head out towards the City Central Library. Turn to **80**.

22

With a lightning manoeuvre, you leap over the edge of the gantry, falling about seven metres. Throw three dice and subtract the total from your STAMINA. If the fall hasn't killed you, you manage to escape the warehouse and thugs.

The only worthwhile clue you have left – as going back to the warehouse would be a bit impractical – is the knowledge that their 'shipment' is coming from the asteroids. You decide to find somebody in the space industry who may know something about illegal space traffic. Turn to **384**.

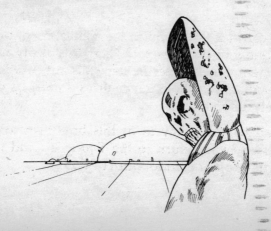

23

To your surprise, he is in! He looks up at you with indifference, as if he is used to people bursting in on him unannounced. You might as well come straight to the point and question him.

Will you act tough to extract the necessary information (turn to **208**), or play 'Mr Nice Guy' (turn to **296**)?

24

The two dead men hang listlessly in the air, their knives floating near by. From several corridors leading into the room come the sounds of pursuit and hysteria. You go back down the corridor you entered by.

Will you go straight back to your spacecraft and thence to Kether (turn to **231**), or down the other passage at the intersection where you heard the monks' voices (turn to **385**)?

25

Sticking your gun barrel against his chest, you push him over to a wall. 'That's just not good enough,' you say. 'I'm afraid I'm going to have to shoot you.' He closes his eyes and grits his teeth – resigned to death? *Test your Luck*. If you are successful, turn to **347**; otherwise turn to **386**.

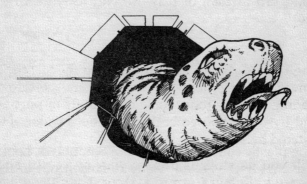

26

The jets flare again, but you have misjudged the angle at which to hold them and find yourself drifting by the satellite at an angle. You'll have to make an adjustment with the jets if you are to make it. Roll two dice. If the result is higher than or equal to your SKILL, turn to **104**. If the result is less than your SKILL, turn to **182**.

27

The turbines whine as you push the accelerator to the floor, and the car shudders as you smash into the rear of the sloop. Your bumpers mangle slightly, but otherwise the collision has little effect. *Test your Luck*. If you are successful, turn to 388; otherwise turn to 349.

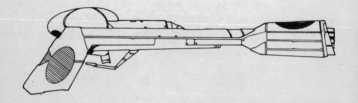

28

The plastic containers are full of Satophil-d. Looks like they were getting ready to ship it out to the mainland. In one of the corners of the room you discover the curled-up body of a man, obviously killed by the teeth of a rather savage beast or at the hands of a skilled torturer. With all the fracas you have recently caused in this room, other guards may be coming. Will you search this man to try to discover why he was killed (turn to 350), or just leave (turn to 389)?

29

You grab the lever, and the iris lock shuts, with a click like a camera shutter. Air rushes back into the room with a roar. Turn to 371.

30

'Hi there!' you shout at a young bar-wench. 'I'm new in town and I'm sort of looking for somebody who can help a young, unscrupulous type of person, like me, get along without having to work in a regular way, see?'

'Oh, yeah?' she shouts back, disdainfully. 'What d'yer do, zero head?' You perform a quick bit of thinking here: what's absolutely essential for a drug-producing outfit?

'I'm a chemist. I make funny little crystals for people to stick in their bloodstreams,' you yell. She blinks at you a bit, obviously thinking without seeing you. Hiking up her skirt she reveals a garter purse. Slapping it, she says, 'Five hundred kopecks, jerk.'

Will you pay her (turn to 323) or not? If you decide not to pay you will just have to mingle with the throng (turn to 362).

31

Having started the eject cycle, your spacecraft begins to disintegrate around you, the debris confusing the attacking craft. The escape pod, of which the bridge is part, begins to perform some violent evasive manoeuvres to bring you safely to the surface of Rispin's End. The attacking craft, obviously convinced that you have been destroyed, break off. You are on the grey, pocked surface of Kether's moon. Leaving the escape pod and setting off on foot towards the dome town, you are distracted only by the odd piece of debris from your ex-spacecraft falling softly to the ground. With the low gravity on this moon, some of the pieces could remain in orbit for days, maybe weeks.

You trek across the moon for hours, taking nine-metre steps until, with alarm, you realize that your oxygen is running low. To your right, nestled at the foot of a crater some kilometres away, you can see a small orange dome, the only sign of possible habitation that you have seen since you ejected.

Will you approach the dome, in the hope that it is occupied (turn to 353), or will you keep going, just in case the dome town is only over the next ridge (turn to 392)?

32

The security guard knocks you into submission, handcuffs you and calls more guards on his com-link. Turn to **129**.

33

'I . . . I'm sorry, I didn't mean to destroy the files,' he pleads.

'What?' you say sarcastically. 'You didn't *mean* to?'

'Oh . . . er . . . well, that's not what I meant . . . er . . . what do you want to know – I was covering up for some flights from the islands . . .'

'Which ones?' you snap.

'I don't know – we only pick them up when they've almost reached the continent's coast . . . but mainly I was covering up for flights to the asteroids.'

'Who were you doing this for?'

'I . . . I don't know . . . I just receive a cheque every month . . .'

He may be lying. If you think he needs a bit more terror to make him come out with the truth, turn to **374**. Otherwise, if you think sheer fright is making him become a bit confused, then go easier on him and turn to **335**.

34

The hatch opens into a small antiseptic airlock. Once through this, however, you find a rough-hewn corridor, dimly lit with yellow arc lights, leading towards the centre of the asteroid. The walls of the corridor have, evidently, been treated with some kind of plastic to prevent the air inside from filtering away into space. Weightless, you follow the corridor until it enters a spherical room. Above you, a tiny niche is cut into the wall – its contents lie in darkness. In front of you the corridor continues out of the room and further into C230. Will you follow the corridor (turn to 336), or examine the niche (turn to 375)?

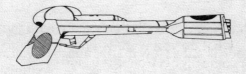

35

The meeting they have arranged for you is with Mrs Torus, wife of Clive Torus, one of their ex-buddies. They take you to the glasshouses in the enormous Botanic Gardens of Kether's capital city.

'The documents,' the punk driver of the black ground-sloop you are in explains, 'are in a safety-deposit box. She'll have them for you.' They park behind a glasshouse, show you where Mrs Torus is standing, and push you from the car. Turn to 376.

36

You take your spacecraft into orbit. If your own spacecraft has been destroyed you will have to hire another for the trip for 1,000 kopecks. After a few days of searching for anything in an L16 orbit, you discover the satellite. Turn to 377.

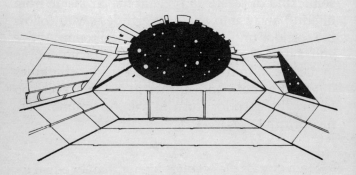

37

The sloop is only a few metres ahead of you when it comes to an S-bend – the big car slops clumsily into the corner, far too fast. Here's your chance! As they go around, will you ram them in the back (turn to 135), or hit them in the side (turn to 396)?

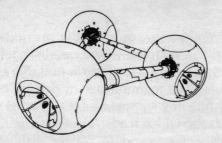

38

The machine drops from the air and explodes into flames. You step past the remnants and proceed along the corridor, coming shortly to an intersection. Will you continue down the corridor (turn to **340**), or take the side-passage (turn to **379**)?

39

Roll two dice. If the result is higher than or equal to your SKILL turn to **302**. If the result is less than your SKILL turn to **341**.

40

The door opens, leading you into the room you were in before. It is pointless to go back. Return to **186**.

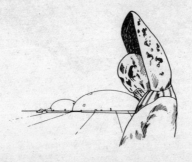

41

After several hours scanning the previous several years' daily news releases and case lists, it becomes evident that there is very little to find. No articles at all on organized manufacture or dealing of drugs, and only one tiny snippet under a case list released four years ago which reads: 'Central Criminal Court 3: State vs. Z. Gross and B. "Blaster" Babbet. Before Justice Zark. Charge: trafficking in illicit organic materials (Satophil-d). Sitting 10.30 a.m.' After that there is nothing. No record of conviction – nothing.

You look them up in the vidiphone directory and find an address for B. Babbet, but nothing for Z. Gross. Will you go and look over B. Babbet's address (turn to 256), or go to the State Computer File Centre to see if anything else about these two can be uncovered (turn to 246)?

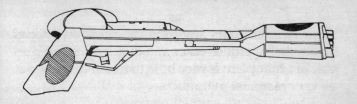

42

As you draw your blaster, he fires at you. You will have to fight him.

GUNMAN   SKILL 6   STAMINA 8

If you defeat him, turn to **13**.

43

You climb the guttering on to the roof and find a window. Roll two dice. If the result is higher than or equal to your SKILL, turn to **82**. If the result is less than your SKILL, turn to **14**.

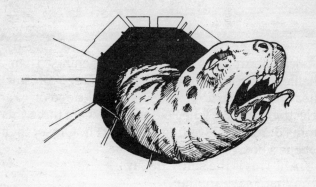

44

You arrive at the meeting-place. The greenhouses in the Botanic Gardens contain a huge, rambling display of exotic plant forms, both native and off-world – a very picturesque spot.

You see Mrs Torus, safety-deposit box sticking out of bag, waiting for you to meet her. She has not seen you yet. Will you look around the grounds first to see if you are being watched (turn to 15), or just go right up and meet her (turn to 376)?

45

A few hours pass with little happening. Then a helijet arrives with a one-tonne cargo of small heavy-duty plastic boxes. These are loaded on to an electric dray and wheeled over to where three Customs officers are waiting to inspect it. One of them opens a box.

'Ah! This is the stuff,' he says.
'What?' says another.
'You know, Satophil-d – dope, stuff, dust.'

'Oh.'

'Anything to declare?' he says to the helijet pilot.

'No. Of course not,' is the reply.

'Very good,' says the Customs official. 'Passed inspection.' He stamps the boxes with a large red sign, saying PASSED CUSTOMS – FOR EXPORT. How blatant can they get in their contempt for the law? Time to put an end to this. You burst out of the locker, drawing your blaster as you go. 'Freeze!' you cry, aiming your gun at the pilot's head. They keep very, very still. You utter a few threats concerning their fates if they don't tell you who is running this racket. They spill the beans.

'The Isosceles Tower . . .' says one Customs official.

'. . . in the city . . .' says another.

'. . . top floor . . .' says the last.

'. . . and don't forget the communications satellite in the L16 orbit . . .' gasps the helijet pilot.

'No . . . we won't,' say the others.

After imprisoning these very guilty felons aboard your spacecraft, will you go to the Isosceles Tower (turn to **320**), or check out the communications satellite (turn to **36**)?

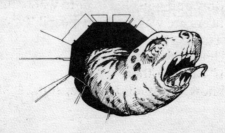

46

The car slides a bit but stays on the road. The sloop has been lost ahead in the thickness of the forest. However, you see a small side-track approaching on the right. Did the sloop continue on the main road or take the track? Which will you take: main road (turn to **329**) or track (turn to **17**)?

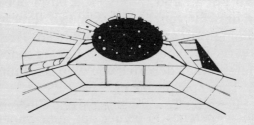

47

Having defeated them, you may claim the first thug's fully automatic blaster, which will cause 6 points of damage every time you hit an opponent.

After the smoke clears you approach the private office and open its door. A tall, gangly bureaucrat attacks you with a paperweight. 'Out, out!' he screams as he swings at you. He has taken you by surprise, so *Test your Luck*. If you are successful, turn to **18**; otherwise turn to **369**.

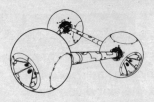

48
You sight up on one of the mines – a flat disk-shaped piece of potential energy just waiting to blow you to atoms – and let fire with your phasers. The mine explodes far more violently than you expected, the impact hitting your ship even from the supposedly safe distance that you chose to fire from. You lose 1 SHIELD. Fortunately, though, thanks to the defenders' incompetence in laying out their minefield, the mine has set off a chain reaction through the rest of the field. They all explode, giving you a clear passage through to the asteroid. Turn to 312.

49
With the alien vanquished, you cross the bridge and go down the exit corridor, coming shortly to a T-junction. Will you turn to the left (turn to 352), or the right (turn to 20)?

50

As you circle around Kether's moon, scanning the surface, you are alerted by your ship's computer to the approach of two small robot fighters. They are swooping up from the far side of Rispin's End, lasers stabbing beams at you! They have cut across your path and there is little chance of escaping them without fighting. As you lock on your defensive screens one question raises itself – Why? You fight them.

	WEAPONS STRENGTH	SHIELDS
ROBOT FIGHTER 1	7	1
ROBOT FIGHTER 2	7	1

If your ship is destroyed, throw one die. If the result is even, you may eject (turn to 31); otherwise you have been destroyed. If you defeat the robots turn to 294.

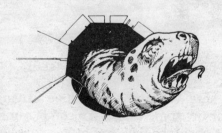

51

You hide on the porch of the apartment block next door – just in time too, for a thin man comes along the street and enters the porch of the woman's building. He speaks on the intercom.

'Zera?'

'Yeah?' comes the crackling, machine-distorted reply.

'It's Arthur.'

'Ah . . . good. Come on up.'

He enters the building and emerges ten minutes later, looks cautiously up and down the street and strides off towards the city centre. Will you follow him (turn to 2) or continue to watch the apartment (turn to 109)?

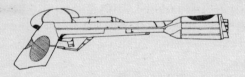

52

They do not see you. 'Everything ready?' one of the men asks.

'Sure, sure. What time's the dope arriving?'

'Tomorrow some time – it's coming in from the asteroids again, so we can't be sure exactly when. Might have re-entry problems.'

'Ah . . .'

They talk for a while about the receiving arrangements and then leave the storeroom. The landing is a little bit too far above the storeroom to make jumping practical, so you go back down the stairs. Will you continue to explore the warehouse by going through the other door (turn to 3), or leave the place and look for somebody in the space industry who may know something about the illegal space traffic you heard the two men discussing (turn to 384)?

53

You swat at the bug, but it flies away and settles on a rafter above you – still watching. You attempt a few manoeuvres – diving into a passing helicab, walking through a crowded shopping-mall, and even running in and out of different elevators. But all this is to no effect, evidently, as you find when you leap out of one elevator and are confronted by two men holding blasters fifteen centimetres from your belly. There is no chance of escaping them, as you'd be blown to pieces from this distance. They lead you out the back of the shop which you were in. Turn to 316.

54

Will you shout a question at the beast (turn to **356**), or just order it to leave you alone (turn to **5**)?

55

'Raise your hands over your head,' warns the security guard, as he walks forward, blaster pointing at your midriff. 'Just what the zark do you think you're up to, Mr Zero?' You raise your hands. Will you demonstrate to him that you are a Federal Narcotics Investigator (turn to **6**), or keep your cover and attempt to bribe him instead (turn to **318**)?

56

Suddenly, the forest is gone. The road, curving in a long wide arc to the right, is clear but for the black sloop which is about 250 metres ahead and hurtling along. Will you drive on the wrong side of the road in an attempt to shorten the distance (turn to **290**), or not (turn to **7**)?

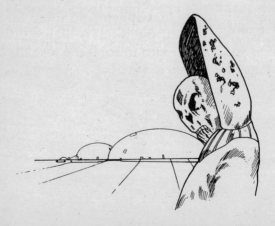

57
But you actually miss it by a few centimetres! It squeals around the curves with you in close pursuit. Turn to 378.

58
Leaving the room by another corridor, you come to a T-junction. To the left and right the corridor splits and heads into dim yellow light before turning from view. Will you go left (turn to 360), or right (turn to 9)?

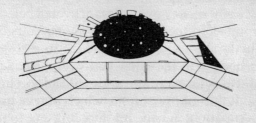

59
You make it to the first sphere and jump for the next. Roll two dice. If the result is higher than or equal to your SKILL, turn to 10. If the result is less than your SKILL, turn to 361.

60

The corridor twists and turns, but you can see him ahead. You pursue him until his path is blocked by an airlock door which he is hastily trying to open. You notice, however, that the warning light above the door is on. There is a vacuum on the other side!

He opens the door and, terror and sudden realization in his eyes, is swept out by a rush of air into the airless reaches of Rispin's End. His body spins slowly in the low gravity over a vast grey plain.

You are also swept forward but, fortunately, the airlock's emergency override is activated before you find yourself in space. The door shuts. You go back to your spaceship, suit up and go to recover the man's body which, when you eventually find it, yields little information – no identification, simply a mechanical component for a helijet. Maybe his normal occupation, when not shooting at strangers, was a mechanic?

There seems to be little point in staying on Rispin's End, so you return to Kether. You can either go to one of the heliports around the capital (turn to **206**), or perhaps do a bit of 'research' at the City Central Library (turn to **80**).

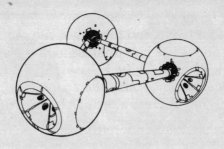

61

The gantry ends in a door, which opens on to the roof. You receive a sudden push in the back which sends you sprawling to your knees. The last thing you hear is the click of a blaster being set off 'safety'. You have failed.

62

There are too many files to look at them all, so you decide to have a look in his desk drawers. Turn to **179**.

63

Drawing your pistol, you float over their heads and say, 'Ahem.' They look up, but seem impervious to the threat that your gun poses to their existence. They merely scream, 'Intruder! Intruder in the monastery!' Then, in the frenzy of their panic, they pull long knives from hidden folds in their garments and try to stab you. 'Kill the infidel!' cries one. 'Death to the unbeliever!' cries the other. They will attack you one at a time rather than simultaneously. You must fight them hand to hand.

	SKILL	STAMINA
MONK 1	9	5
MONK 2	7	5

If you defeat them, turn to **24**.

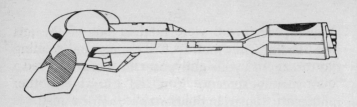

64

'Don't shoot me, please!' he whispers. 'I'll tell . . . tell you what I know.' You take a few menacing steps towards him. 'You do that,' you say, encouragingly.

'There are some intermittent transmissions we get from a . . . a satellite in orbit. An L16 orbit, I think. They tell us when to expect a . . . a shipment . . . but . . . but . . .' he stutters.

'But what?'

'Oh . . . er . . . but nothing really, that's it.'

Maybe he's telling the truth. You could go out into space and check up on this satellite (turn to **36**), or you could assume that he knows some more and rough him up a bit to see what else he'll say (turn to **25**).

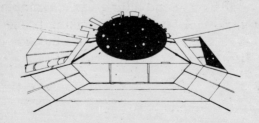

65

You find that you were holding one of the jets incorrectly, cutting off its fuel supply and sending yourself spinning slightly. You have only covered a quarter of the distance. You'll have to have another shot with the jets. Roll two dice. If the result is higher than or equal to your SKILL, turn to **26**. If the result is less than your SKILL, turn to **260**.

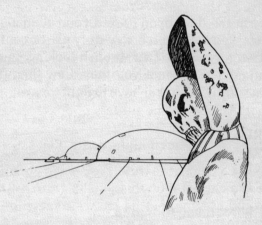

66

They swerve wildly across the road before fishtailing over the verge and hitting a tree, wrapping the car around it. A bit of harsh braking brings your own car to a more civilized halt on the side of the road. Turn to **359**.

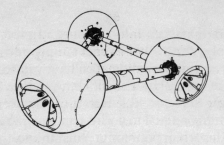

67

You push the door open to find yourself in a large room stacked high with heavy-duty plastic containers. There are also four brutish-looking guards present. When they see you they draw their guns and start firing. You will have to fight them.

	SKILL	STAMINA
GUARD 1	7	6
GUARD 2	6	6
GUARD 3	5	4
GUARD 4	5	4

If you defeat them, turn to **28**.

68

You fly towards it, but miss by millimetres. Clawing frantically, you grapple with the edge of the airlock, but the rush of air is too strong and sweeps you into space. You have failed.

69

The figure smashes into a thousand pieces when you shoot it. The other Babbet laughs, turns to the left and opens fire, enigmatically, away from you. To your horror, blaster shells come tearing through the folding screen and smash into your body. The figures were reflections! The gangster was hiding behind the screen all along. You sink to the floor, your wounds making an irremovable stain in the plush pile of the carpet. You have failed.

70

The woman seems to remain unaware of your presence and, after a short time, enters a five-storey apartment block. A few moments after entering, a fourth-floor light comes on. You go up to the block's porch and look at the residents' list. Five names – one per floor, probably. The fourth floor is occupied by

ZERA GROSS
STELLAR AND INTERPLANETARY
IMPORT/EXPORT

Will you stay and watch her apartment (turn to 51), or call it a day and spend the morrow searching in the City Central Library for some information about this Zera Gross (turn to 80)?

71

As soon as you land on the floor, a flashlight is on you. 'Stop!' a voice cries. You can't afford to be caught here in this position, so you will have to fight the security guard who has discovered you. You can't start a gun fight either, because the noise of blaster shots would certainly attract more guards. You dive at him and fight hand to hand.

	SKILL	STAMINA
SECURITY GUARD	10	8

If you defeat him, ignore any damage that he inflicted upon you (the damage is only temporary) and turn to **119**. If you lose, turn to **32**.

72

'Please don't send me to jail,' he pleads. 'I've told you everything!'

'What about the Customs officer's name?' you ask.

'Zac – Zac Kalensus,' he says. 'He pays me to do it . . . but I won't any more . . .'

'Yeah . . . yeah,' you say. Turn to **111**.

73

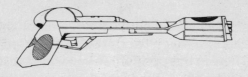

73

You rocket out to asteroid C230. If your own spacecraft has been destroyed, you will have to pay out 2,000 kopecks to hire another for the trip.

C230 is about 300 metres in diameter, with the only signs of habitation being a dock and a few antennae. Seems to be fairly quiet, though – at least your arrival hasn't resulted in the launching of any anti-shipping missiles . . . yet.

You don your pressure-suit and space-walk around the outside of the rock, discovering, seemingly, only three ways of entering: the dock area, a small emergency entry hatch, and an air-conditioning radiator vent. Entering via the dock would be a bit obvious, so will you try the hatch (turn to **34**), or the vent (turn to **229**)?

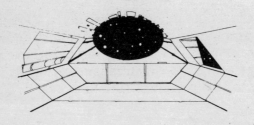

74

You miss! Startled, he turns to see you and begins to shout into a walk-phone. As you take aim again, he slides from the tree, taking a potshot as he goes, and hitting you in the hand. Subtract 1 from your SKILL. Other shots can be heard now, and a woman's screams. Chasing the sniper, you see Mrs Torus's blaster-riddled body lying next to the black sloop that you saw parked behind the glasshouse. The sniper picks up the safety-deposit box Mrs Torus had been carrying for you, and dives into the sloop, which squeals off. Will you try and give chase to the car (turn to **191**), or stop and tender aid to Mrs Torus (turn to **210**)?

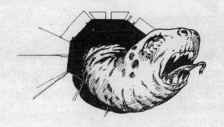

75

In the city, you visit a lot of cheap dives, a few of the places you were at before, and ask a lot of questions – all to no avail. Everything seems to have gone underground. The organization has finally been alerted to your presence. Turn to **16**.

76

You pursue the sloop through the forest, your bumpers almost touching. Suddenly, the forest disappears and the road is in the open, going up a raised embankment. Will you try to draw up next to them (turn to **310**), or ram them from behind (turn to **27**)?

77

You pass down the corridor and come to an intersection. Will you continue down the corridor (turn to **340**), or turn up the side-passage (turn to **379**)?

78

You shoot at it, while it tries to engulf you in electric fire.

	SKILL	STAMINA
SENTINEL	7	10

If you destroy it, turn to **263**.

79

A small poisoned dart, fired from a minuscule opening in a corner, hits you. The door does not open. Lose 1 point of STAMINA. Return to **186**.

80

The City Central Library is an enormous complex, housing millions of volumes of vidis, microfilms and even a few books. It is almost devoid of human life when you arrive: there is no organic staff and most subscribers get the information or volumes they want sent to them by cable. You seat yourself at a terminal marked FOR PUBLIC USE ONLY.

Will you start by looking through old vidinews for something on local organized crime (turn to **41**), or look up some government-released statistics instead (turn to **12**)?

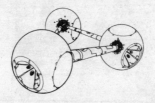

81

The café owner doesn't recall the name and has not seen anyone, other than those you saw, enter the premises. Disgruntled, you leave the café.

'Oi, you!' calls a voice behind you. Turning, you see that it is a clean-cut looking fellow pointing a blaster at you. 'Come here.' He waves the gun menacingly.

Will you attempt to run from him (turn to **364**), or draw your own blaster and threaten him back (turn to **42**)?

82

As you open the window, an alarm begins sounding. Footsteps can be heard approaching from the garden and behind the window. Trapped! Two guards appear. You will have to shoot at them.

	SKILL	STAMINA
GUARD 1	8	6
GUARD 2	6	6

If you defeat them, you are forced, by the presence of more guards, to leave the manor-house altogether. Turn to **231**.

83

Cautiously, you approach the pedestal and flame. It roars brighter. The doors slam shut! You see a monstrous serpentine figure with a woman's face forming in the flame over the pedestal. It sprouts a couple of dozen scaly legs from behind its face, turns blue and begins to laugh. You notice that its mouth is full of steel fangs. A couple of leather wings grow from its back. The beast reaches and grabs you with a few of its legs.

If you have read the prayer to Thuvald, you may recite it (turn to 122). Otherwise, you will either have to shoot the beast (turn to 93), or try to speak with it (turn to 54).

84

The guard moves down the row of lockers, finally reaching yours. He puts his hand on the latch.

'Hey, Harry!' a voice within the depot cries. 'Time for a beer, ol' buddy.'

'Is that so?' says the security guard, looking at his watch. 'Guess it is, too.'

Leaving your locker, he strolls off in the direction of his friend. Safe! Turn to 45.

85

You hurtle into the forest at well over 200 k.p.h., to find the road curving in tight S-bends between thick clumps of trees. You fight with the steering-wheel to keep the car on the road. Roll two dice. If the result is higher than or equal to your SKILL, turn to **270**. If the result is less than your SKILL, turn to **46**.

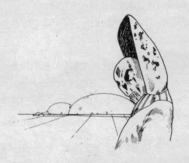

86

You enter a small ante-room to a private office. Standing by an enormous wooden table, pushing piles of files through a shredding-machine and tossing magnetic memory into a little incinerator on the wall, are two brutish-looking characters. They are both armed. When they see you, they dive to the floor and begin firing. One of them is armed with a fully automatic blaster.

	SKILL	STAMINA
THUG 1	10	6
THUG 2	6	6

If you defeat them, turn to **47**.

87

You return to the mainland and then rocket out to the asteroid belt. If your own spacecraft has been destroyed, you will have to hire another at a cost of 2,000 kopecks. If you cannot afford this then you have failed.

When you approach the environs of the drug runners' asteroid, the command screen on your ship flashes a message: MINEFIELD SURROUNDING TARGET. You look out to see a thickly clustered globular minefield set around the production asteroid – a very tricky proposition.

Will you shoot your way through the mines (turn to **48**), or carefully manoeuvre through instead (turn to **19**)?

88

You fire at each other.

	SKILL	STAMINA
ARCTURIAN VANQUE	7	10

If you defeat it, turn to **49**.

89

You go to the main heliport where the Air-traffic Chief works. Now, should you follow him home from work to confront him (turn to **247**), or try to get into his office when he's not there (turn to **257**)?

90

You come back to the centre when it is dark – not that it being dark has that much relevance to your chances of being detected, but at least most of the staff should be away. You don't even attempt to go over the razor wire – certain detection there. Instead, you climb up a drainpipe on the pillbox set aside for public inquiries. You reach the roof. From here you climb along an insulated cable, which runs between the pillbox and the main building, until you are on the roof of the actual centre. You open a skylight and drop into the building. *Test your Luck*. If you are successful, turn to **119**; otherwise turn to **71**.

91

Your foes are dead. As you step from the warehouse, with the sounds of pursuit close behind you, another thug steps out from behind the pile of rubbish by the back door. You spin round and raise your blaster. 'No, wait!' he implores, holding a piece of paper out to you. You hesitate, take the paper, and then sprint from the environs of the warehouse. Later you read the note:

> *Dear Narc,*
> *Meet me at the Café Heroes of the*
> *Federation, 9.00 a.m. tomorrow.*
> *Yours unhappily in crime,*
> *Clive Torus*

You might as well meet him. Turn to **315**.

92

While sitting in a sleazy bar, talking to a hoary old asteroid miner, you notice a buzzing little insect land on your shoulder. You go to brush it off but – *freeze* – that's no insect. That's a bug, an electronic bug. Though minutely fashioned to look like an insect, you can see, at close examination, the tiny jets under the mock wings, and the vidicamera for an eye – an eye that is staring straight into your own.

Will you try to lose the bug (turn to 53) or ignore it and go to the starport to conduct your inquiries (turn to 345)?

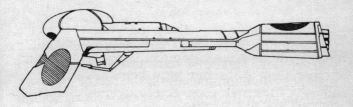

93

You draw your pistol and begin pumping shots into the beast's head and body. It laughs, draws itself to its full height, pounces – and swallows you whole. You have failed.

94

You sprint from the depot. The guard gets off one shot at you, but misses. Well, you won't be able to do anything around the starport for a while, so you head off to find another lead. Turn to 231.

95

You follow the road for about ten kilometres, but there is no sign of the villains. You have lost them. Disconsolate, you drive back into the city. Turn to **16**.

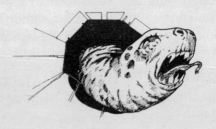

96

The duty proctor, smoothing the wrinkles from his uniform, hurries along a short corridor, beckoning you to follow. He shows you into a large office filled mainly by an enormous desk, the rest of the space being taken by the huge investigator sitting behind it.

'Hello,' you say, after the duty proctor has left, 'I'm a Grade 1 Investigator from Federal Central (Vice). I've been sent here to crack the Aleph Cygni drug ring and would appreciate any information or aid you can give me.'

'Why certainly, dear chap,' he says jovially. 'Here, have a cigar – Vegan, you know.' He lights up before continuing, 'I would love to be of assistance but, you see, there is no Aleph Cygni drug ring.'

'What?'

'Fiction. We have absolutely no evidence of anything large-scale, only one small operation out on Rispin's End, but that could hardly supply a granny, let alone export to other worlds! Ha, ha!'

'So, the only operation you know about is on the moon?'

'Yes, that's it.' His jolly face is beaming at you. 'You could go and take a look out there, but I should hardly bother.'

'Oh?'

'No, no. I believe you've been sent on a wild-goose chase. Dear, oh dear, these Federal fellows, if you'll excuse my rudeness, wouldn't know a drug ring from a Scallopian Fang.'

Perhaps not. There is obviously a source of, to use politician's jargon, misinformation about. Federal or local? Well, regardless of this man's views on Federal efficiency, you must continue the investigation until matters are resolved to your satisfaction. Will you go to Rispin's End (turn to **398**), or ignore the local proctors and continue by searching for some bar or dive where someone might give a clue or two away (turn to **299**)?

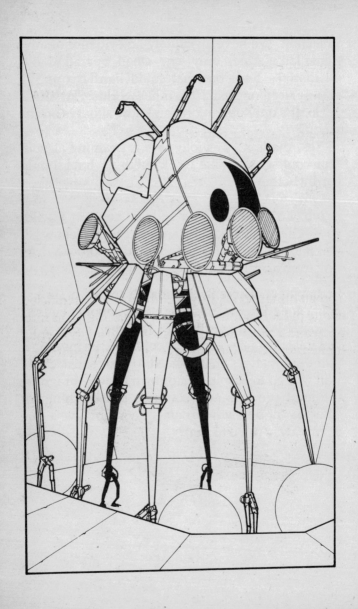

97

You shoot it out.

	SKILL	STAMINA
ANTARIAN ROBOT	8	8

If you defeat it, turn to 58.

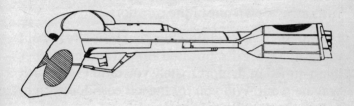

98

You go off target slightly, drifting into the tentacles of one of the bulbous creatures. The thing turns into teeth and a cavernous maw, snapping wildly at you. It bites you. Lose 4 points of STAMINA. Turn to 59.

99

Walking through the spacious corridors of the dome town, deep in thought, you accidentally bump into a person rounding a corner. 'Excuse me,' you say, glancing . . . it's him! The assassin! Recognizing you, he swings the bag he is carrying – probably with his rifle in it – and knocks you off balance. He runs away down one of the corridors.

In a moment you are after him, but he is already out of sight, having disappeared around another corner at a T-junction. Unfortunately you didn't see which way he went. Will you try the left corridor (turn to **60**), or the right (turn to **21**)?

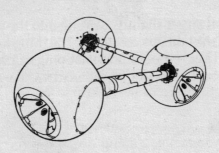

100

You raise your arms above your head as the gunmen close in. The car door opens and out steps this shifty-looking dude. He walks up to you slowly, thoughtfully.

'Who . . . who are you?' you ask, trying not to sound too frightened.

'My friends,' he says, searching you casually, 'call

me "Blaster", but to you, it doesn't matter.' He doesn't find your gun.

'Why not?'

'Ha . . . because, my friend, you are about to die. We are expecting a shipment from the asteroids tonight, see? As a consequence of your snooping you must, alas . . .' Here he draws his finger across his throat.

'OK, boys,' he says to the gunmen. 'On the roof, three bullets in the head.' You are led by two of them up a staircase and along a gantry towards the roof of the warehouse. As you walk along the raised gantry several options present themselves to you. You could try grabbing a rafter and kicking the thugs off the gantry (turn to **383**); or you could just jump off the gantry yourself and hope the fall doesn't kill or cripple you (turn to **22**); or you could wait a while longer and hope that a better opportunity of escape presents itself (turn to **61**).

101

You hear someone coming down the corridor towards the office. Quickly, you step outside, smile at the young lady standing there and say, 'He doesn't seem to be in.' You stride past her and out of the building. The asteroid known as C230 should be no problem to find, so will you take a trip out to look at it (turn to **73**), or try to find somebody in the space industry who can verify the fact of illegal traffic out to the asteroids (turn to **384**)?

102

You float cautiously into the hall and take up a place behind a row of black-clad figures, who are thronging the hall. They begin to chant and sway. A couple of men out in front swing burning incense in great circles. Soon a man, obviously the MC or high priest, appears out in front and begins a long prayer to some holy malevolence known as Thuvald. Obviously you have the wrong place – this is a monastery, a weird one no doubt, but still a monastery. You sneak out of the hall, away from C230 and head back to the Kether. Turn to **231**.

103

He freezes. 'I . . . I don't know . . .' he stutters. You wave your pistol and take a couple of menacing steps towards him.' . . . very much . . . just about some transmissions from a satellite in orbit . . . an L16 orbit, I think. Please don't shoot me!' You threaten him a bit more but with little effect. Perhaps that is all he knows. You decide to have a look in space for this satellite. Turn to **36**.

104

You drop the jets! They fire continuously, exhausting themselves of fuel and dragging you, via the safety wires attaching yourself to them, in the wrong direction. You spin off into space. You have failed.

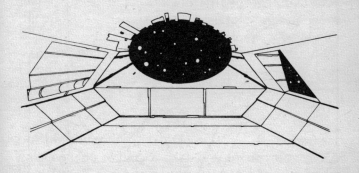

105

You didn't quite hit them hard enough – they manage to regain control and stay on the road. The collision did, however, cost you a bit of speed. Turn to **46**.

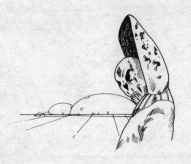

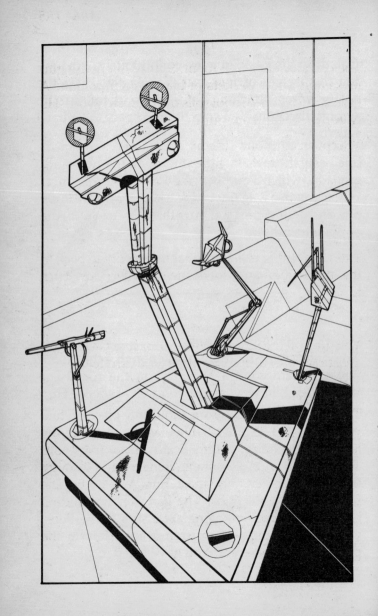

106

The corridor ends in a room. Spread about are gun racks and a few packets of blaster ammunition. A little gun-cleaning robot rolls over towards you. 'Hi! Nice day. Clean your gun?'

You push it to one side as you enter the room. A brief search reveals little more than one hand-grenade, which you keep. You may use this once. When you use it against a foe (or foes), throw three dice and deduct the total from the STAMINA of *all* the opponents present.

There's nothing else in the room, so you go back to the intersection and down the main corridor. Turn to 340.

107

You jump at the large red lever. *Test your Luck*. If you are successful, turn to 29; otherwise turn to 68.

108

The figure smashes into a thousand pieces when you shoot it. The other Babbet laughs, turns to the left and opens fire, enigmatically, away from you. To your horror, blaster shells come tearing through the folding screen and smash into your body. The figures were reflections! The gangster was hiding behind the screen all along. You sink to the floor, your wounds making an irremovable stain in the plush pile of the carpet. You have failed.

109

You take up station just across the road in the shadow of a shop doorway. The light on the fourth floor goes out after fifteen minutes. Nothing happens for about five minutes; then, with no warning, six huge – *really* huge – thugs come out of nowhere to confront you.

"Ere, you, Vanque head.'

'What?' you say.

'This . . .' They grab you and, as they say, proceed to beat you to a pulp. Eventually, they leave you alone. After recovering consciousness some time later, you drag yourself off to receive some medical attention and rest. Lose 2 STAMINA points permanently. With the new day, you head off to the library to look up Z. Gross. Turn to **80**.

110

'Hey, you, stop!' one of the men yells, as you move towards the stairs. Damn! Seen. You go down the stairs, open the door, and are confronted by another two men with drawn blasters. You will have to fight them.

	SKILL	STAMINA
THUG 1	6	8
THUG 2	5	8

If you defeat them, turn to **91**.

111

'Today, in fact,' he continues, 'some stuff arrived . . . and will probably go through Customs tomorrow.' Well, you don't know exactly where the stuff is coming from, so there's no point in flying out to the islands yet. So will you pay customs a visit on the morrow (turn to 337), or try to find someone else in the space industry who may know about illegal traffic (turn to 384)?

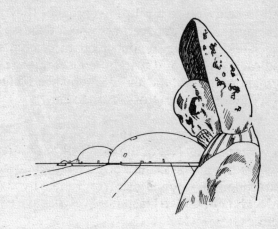

112

'Ha!' you say defiantly. 'You don't scare me!'
'Pity,' she says. 'OK, Brak an' Johnny?'
'Yeah?'
'Kill the dummy.'

This is the end of the road. The last thing you hear or see is Brak cocking his gun before pulling the trigger. You have failed.

113

The driver, in response to your frantic waving, pulls over to the side of the road. 'What?' he asks in astonishment when you drag him from the car. 'Hey . . . wait!' he yells, when you hurl his vehicle into a wide arc and set off after the escaping villains. Looks like you've had a bit of luck, anyway, as the ground car you are in is a small, powerful six-wheeled sport model with twin gas turbines. Should be able to pull a few hundred kilometres an hour with this.

You flick on the traffic radar – picking the sloop up ahead – and accelerate to 200 k.p.h. If you stopped to shoot before waving this car down, turn to **387**; otherwise turn to **202**.

114

After a few more days of non-discovery you give up and return to Kether to look the city over for possible leads. Turn to **75**.

115

The turbines give a magnificent amount of power, pushing you effortlessly down the slope to within three metres of the sloop. You start pounding on your horn to unnerve them. The two cars dive into a wood. The road becomes quite curvy, necessitating a reduction in speed. You could try to ram the car from behind and send it into a tree – it is a heavier vehicle than yours and will probably be harder to control in these conditions. Will you try to push it off the road (turn to **222**), or not (turn to **76**)?

116

It digests your guess and then fires its blasters at you. 'Wrong one, buddy,' it cackles. You will have to fire at it.

	SKILL	STAMINA
ROBOT SENTRY	8	4

If you defeat it, turn to **38**.

117

You slide your ship into the main dock area, parking next to an interplanetary shuttle. When you open the airlock you find a small spherical droid in front of you. Little rockets on its surface send it darting from side to side while it fires at you with pulsing red lasers. You will have to fire at it.

	SKILL	STAMINA
DEFENCE DROID	9	4

If you defeat it, turn to **156**.

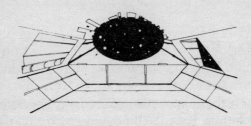

118

You receive an electric shock from the door. It does not open. Lose 1 point of STAMINA and then return to **225**.

119

You are in an office area and there, not two metres from you, is a video link to the Centre's files. Hastily, you begin to retrieve information from it. Turn to **393**.

120

'Yes, of course you can look,' she says. 'All his other papers were kept in the drawer over there.' She points to a bureau. You leaf through the few scraps that lie in the bottom of the drawer – a catalogue of home appliances, a few notes to himself to remind him to pick up dinner or such, a couple of bills, invoices for various harmless articles and one piece of print-out which looks like it came from a telex:

000561402
UAB: QUERT SATCOM XX597134XX END
UAX: CUT

The interesting thing about this print-out is the hand-scrawled message on the back:

Zera,
   Kalensus says he wants a bigger drink
   for his Customs boys.

Clive

Of course the Customs would be in it. This Kalensus must be their boss. Will you meet Mrs Torus later when she has had time to get the documents from the bank (turn to **44**), or pay the Customs a visit and lean heavily on this guy Kalensus (turn to **142**)?

121

You discover an alarm which would have been triggered had you simply opened the window. You easily disarm it. Climbing through the window, you find a short corridor which ends in a tiny bare room. Turn to **365**.

122

As the beast towers over you, you remember what was written on the plaque, and scream it out:

'Hidden is he,
Mighty is he,
His time returns,
Hold, wait, be still!'

The monster hovers in the air and begins a weird ululating cry:

'Misled you have been,
In the wrong place, you are,
With the Customs officials you should be!'

Turn to **161**.

123

You make it. The guard checks the locker you were in and moves on down the row. Eventually he leaves the area altogether. Turn to **357**.

124

The villains' sloop is only ninety metres away when it disappears from sight in a wood. The trees are thick and low – it is impossible to tell whether the road will remain relatively straight or not.

Will you try to close the gap by accelerating (turn to 85), or play it safe by staying the same speed (turn to 76)?

125

The files are useless, but the vidilink, once you work out how to turn it on, is a goldmine. It flashes up one message continually:

> **** ATTENTION ALL STAFF****
> THE FEDS ARE ON TO US SO DESTROY ALL FILES
> INCLUDING THIS MESSAGE. RENDEZVOUS –
> PARADISE, 34 16' 42" WEST, 16 00' 01" NORTH AT
> 21:30. BE EFFICIENT.
>
> ZERA GROSS + BLASTER BABBET.

Good-oh! Later, after you have left the office, it turns out that the co-ordinates are those of a tiny island some 4,000 kilometres off the coast of the mainland. Turn to 330.

126

You leave the room via another door and find yourself in what is obviously a command room – huge vidiscreens and floor-to-ceiling computer banks adorn the walls. Vidilinks are set around at irregular intervals. It all ticks over and flashes quietly to itself. The screens show production figures of Satophil-d in tonnes per month; arrival and departure times of helijet flights between the island and mainland; and the exact location of the asteroid on which all of the drugs are manufactured. This is obviously not the complete operation: what you need to take out now is the production asteroid. Turn to **87**.

127

You take out a few tablets of the drug and dodge towards the bridge, bright gashes of electrons dancing around you. When you are close to the alien, you throw the Satophil-d into its gapingly huge mouth and duck back to the door. The monster stops firing, chews a bit, squats on its haunches and then slips over into the pit. Turn to **49**.

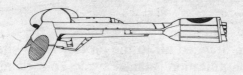

128

The man is busy stripping bits and pieces from one of the helijet's motors when you approach and speak to him. 'Quiet day, isn't it?' you say. He grins and continues to work: 'Yep, sure is. Rest of the week, though, it's go, go, go.' You continue in this vein for a few more minutes before you mention that you've heard that a lot of illegal air traffic comes through here undetected.

'Ha! Undetected my foot. Those guys in traffic control just don't report it.' He pulls a large section of motor out. 'And not just here either. Over at the other heliport, by the starport, they're just as bad.'
  'Oh?'
  'Yup, somebody's hiding something. Probably the Air-traffic Chief over at the starport – everything goes through him.'

Well, whole new avenues! You can try and verify this man's information by doing some research, either at the City Library (turn to **80**), or the State Computer File Centre (turn to **246**). Or you could go to air-traffic control, either at this heliport (turn to **167**) or at the starport (turn to **89**).

129

You are dragged off to the proctor HQ, where all your identification is taken away. Your claims that you are a Federal Investigator fall on deaf ears. Eventually, you are tried, and sent to prison. You have failed.

130

You throw the chief around the room so hard that he stumbles and falls. Leaning over him, you insert your blaster's barrel in one of his ears. 'Now, if you don't tell me everything you know, you might not even make it as far as the jailhouse. Just disappear,' you whisper.

'No . . . no . . . the Customs officer – Zac Kalensus – he pays me to do it . . . and I think there are some files for a few space flights to and from the asteroids that . . . that I have to destroy too . . . not just from the islands.' Turn to **111**.

131

You hang around in the city, frequenting bars, dives, cheap hotels and even looking for likely persons in the vidiphone directory. *Test your Luck*. If you are successful, turn to **4**; otherwise turn to **92**.

132

Just as you reach the exit, the doors slam shut with a terrific *Boom*. Oh, oh. Trapped! Turning, you see a monstrous serpentine figure with a woman's face forming in the flame over the pedestal. It sprouts a couple of dozen scaly legs from behind its face, turns blue and begins to laugh at you. You notice that its mouth is full of steel fangs. A couple of leather wings grow from its back. Frantically, but vainly, you try to open the doors. The beast leaves the flame, advances towards you, and grabs you with a few of its legs. Will you shoot at it (turn to 93), or try to speak with it (turn to 54)?

133

Unknown to you, your jacket has caught on a spring in the door of the locker. *Ping*, it goes, when you accidentally pull it free. 'Hey, you,' says the guard, noticing you, 'stop!' He is drawing his blaster. Will you stop (turn to 55), or run (turn to 94)?

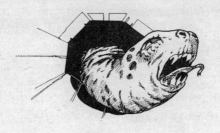

134

Slowing down, you maintain control. The car stays on the road, although it squeals around the corners. You have lost sight of the villains' sloop in the trees. A side-road approaches to the right. Did they go down this or continue on the main road? Will you go down the side-road (turn to 95), or straight on (turn to 56)?

135

Your car leaps forward and smashes into the rear of the sloop, giving the necessary impetus to send it out of control. It fishtails off the road and then flips over and over and over, violently rolling to a halt a hundred metres further on. You pull over to the side of the road. Turn to 359.

136

Your choice is wrong, evidently, as the machine opens fire on you. Turn to 97.

137

Roll two dice. If the result is higher than or equal to your SKILL, turn to **98**. If the result is less than your SKILL, turn to **59**.

138

You take a dive down a narrow alley and sprint away, leaving the assassin behind. However, you did manage to catch a good look at his face – good enough to recognize him if you saw him again. So you go to the dome town's starport and, finding the Arrivals desk unattended, slip behind it, seat yourself at the passport vidilink, and look through all the recent arrivals. There he is! Arrived about a week ago – a Mr B. Smith; age, 34; occupation, librarian; place of work, City Central Library . . .

'Ahem,' says a voice behind you, 'what do you . . .?'

'Sorry,' you say, quickly flashing your Federal Investigator badge at the Arrivals clerk, 'police . . . er . . . proctor matters.'

Will you continue your search on Rispin's End (turn to **99**), or go back to Kether for a bit of research at the library there (turn to **80**)?

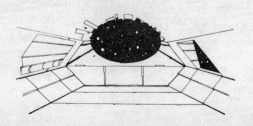

139

As soon as you begin to move, they fire. The deadly hail hits you, and forces you to the ground. You have failed.

140

There are a lot of files, so you pick a few out at random. Only one of them yields anything interesting. It is concerned with an asteroid known as C230 and the occurrence of a fairly large amount of unauthorized traffic between it and Kether. The file does not state or hypothesize any possible reasons for this. Throw a die. If the result is even, turn to **101**; if odd, turn to **62**.

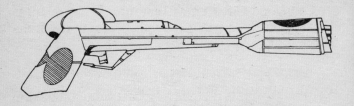

141

You float cautiously into the hall and take up a place behind a row of black-clad figures, who throng the hall. 'Here,' says one of them, noticing you. 'Who are you?' The others, turning to see, move rapidly, seize you and bear you to the front of the hall. 'A toy! A toy!' is chanted throughout. A short while later you lose your life in a rather peculiar religious ceremony. You have failed.

142

You find the office of the Head Customs Officer. ZAC KALENSUS, it says on a little brass plate next to the entrance. You turn the door-handle and kick it open. Standing next to an open window is Mr Kalensus, memo in hand, surprise on his face. You point your pistol at him and say, icily, 'OK, Zac baby, start talking about this little drug racket you're in on or I'll have to start pumping with my trigger finger.' *Test your Luck.* If you are successful, turn to **64**; otherwise turn to **103**.

143

You manage to draw yourself to a halt only a short distance from the satellite. Another short burst and you should reach it. Roll two dice. If the result is higher than or equal to your SKILL, turn to **104**. If the result is less than your SKILL, turn to **221**.

144

Your bumper hits them firmly, catapulting the sloop towards the side of the road. *Test your Luck.* If you are successful, turn to **66**; otherwise turn to **105**.

145

The monster is dead. Stepping past its body, you find yourself at an intersection in a corridor. The main passage continues straight on, while a narrower corridor goes to the right. Which way? Straight on (turn to **340**), or right (turn to **106**)?

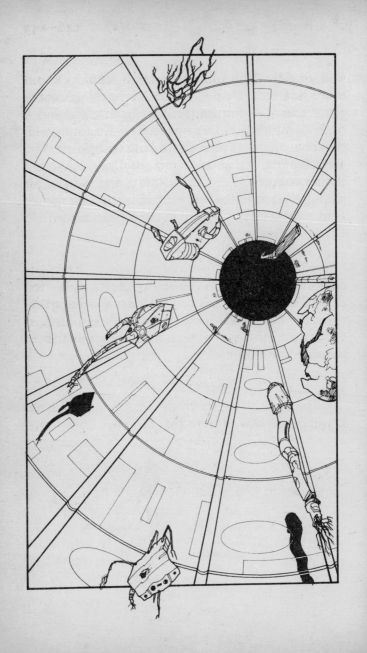

146

You go down the tunnel, through an airlock and into a tiny cone-shaped room. An iris airlock at the other end – which happens to be the big end – opens, revealing empty space! The atmosphere in the room begins to rush out, taking you with it. You are in a garbage disposal room. Will you hold on to the airlock door behind you until the rush of air stops (turn to **390**), or make a dive for the emergency stop lever next to the open iris lock (turn to **107**)?

147

You jump through the folding screen. Babbet is standing behind it, facing the opposite wall – the two figures were simply reflections of the real article in hiding. You tackle him. The two of you roll across the thick carpet, wrestling and trading punches in hand-to-hand combat.

	SKILL	STAMINA
'BLASTER' BABBET	10	8

If you defeat him, turn to **400**.

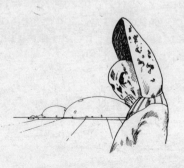

148

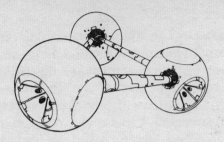

148

You give chase. The woman, despite her weight and age, is quite fast – not fast enough, though. You run in the shadows and it becomes evident, after a couple of minutes, that she believes she has lost you. She goes once around the block and then darts into a five-storey apartment building. A few moments later a light comes on on the fourth floor. Stepping up to the block's porch, you consult the residents' address list. Just five names, one per floor. The fourth floor is taken by a ZERA GROSS, IMPORT/EXPORT.

You can either wait outside the apartment to see if anything develops (turn to **109**), or you could call it a day and spend tomorrow doing a bit of research at the City Central Library to find out a bit more about this Zera Gross (turn to **80**).

149

The door opens on to some stairs. You climb them and find yourself on a raised freight landing; above are doors for a helijet to enter the building and below is a storehouse. A door in the storehouse opens and two men enter. Will you lie down in an attempt to remain hidden (turn to 52), or try to escape from the landing by going back down the stairs (turn to 110)?

150

The block is almost completely deserted. However, you do manage to find two off-duty pilots hanging around the Flight Service Centre.

'What?' they say, cowering, when you ask them about the existence of any illegal space traffic.

'Don't know a thing,' says one.

'Nothing,' says the other.

'Well,' says the first to the second. 'I must be off!'

'Yes,' replies number two, 'so must I!' They scoot off down a corridor.

Very unsatisfactory. Will you continue your inquiries at the starport hangars (turn to 306), or in the city (turn to 189)?

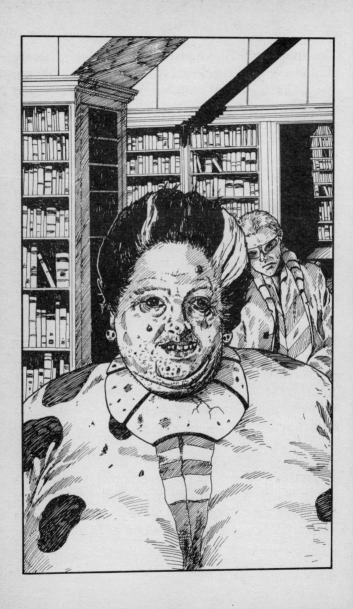

151

You find yourself in a plush room – either a library or a study. Books on real wooden shelves line the walls. There is real wooden furniture, heavy and smoky with long years. Behind a massive desk sits an equally massive but certainly uglier woman. She smiles, gap-toothed, at you. 'You gave us quite a turn, you did, dropping out of space all unexpected like. Isn't that so, boys?' She looks around at the other gangsters who are lolling about on the rest of the furniture, cigarettes dangling from their lips, and bleary, boozy eyes fixed disinterestedly on you.

'Yeah,' they answer.

'We don't have Federal Investigators visiting our little planet at all often. Do we, boys?' she asks again.

'Nah.'

Suddenly, she leans forward, staring at you. Her voice is icy: 'You have two choices, Narc. Either you go to a meeting that we've arranged for you, to pick up a box of documents for us, or else . . .' Will you agree to go to the meeting (turn to **35**), or take the 'or else' (turn to **112**)?

152

Kneeling, you fire half a dozen quick shots at the sloop before it disappears over a hill. Missed! You still have time, though, to wave the other car to a stop and commandeer it for a chase. Turn to **113**.

153

For a few days you have your computer eavesdrop on all the electromagnetic traffic transmitted through space by artificial means. While your ship is doing this, you make a visual search of the surface of Kether. On the fifth day your computer alerts you to the presence of a large communications satellite in an L16 orbit. It receives signals irregularly and transmits a response shortly after – not to the source of the incoming signal but towards Kether. It uses a unidirectional antenna for transmission, but some leakage allowed your computer to detect it.

The suspicious part is the size of the satellite, its infrequent use and the fact that it always transmits to only one building in Kether's capital city. It could be a Defence Department satellite, but . . . Will you go and look at it (turn to 377), or disregard it and continue your surveillance (turn to 114)?

154

The sloop is now 100 metres ahead and accelerating through a wide curve before a long straight. On the left you can see a side-road approaching – it may afford a slight short cut to the straight that the sloop is heading for. Will you take this side-road (turn to 261), or remain on the main road (turn to 202)?

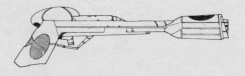

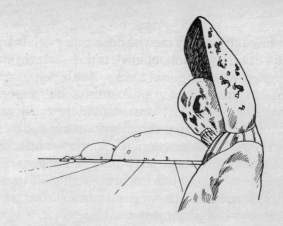

155
Turn to **116**.

156
The sparking remains of the droid float in the vacuum. You leave the sparse dock area via an airlock and proceed towards the centre of the asteroid through a zero-gravity tunnel. Turn to **195**.

157
You receive an electric shock from the door. It does not open. Lose 1 point of STAMINA and then return to **225**.

158

Under a hefty shoulder, the door collapses. Inside, on the floor, in a pool of blood, is the man you were supposed to meet – shot. His eyes open and he crooks a finger at you in an attempt to call you over. 'Beware,' he whispers when you are closer. 'Beware of . . . of Zera Gross and . . . and . . . Blaster B . . .' He expires, the last words too much for him. You search his body and find a wallet and a letter. The wallet identifies the man as being Arthur Flange of no fixed address. The letter is from a friend or acquaintance of his. It reads:

Dear Arthur,
   Re our plans. Z. doesn't suspect yet. We must work out the final details. Meet me at the Café Heroes of the Federation on Thursday at 9 a.m.
   Clive Torus

Will you go to meet Clive tomorrow in place of Arthur (turn to **315**), or go to the City Central Library to look up this Zera Gross that Arthur mentioned – her name might be raised in a case list somewhere (turn to **80**)?

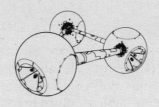

159
You arrange to meet Mrs Torus by the greenhouses in the Botanic Gardens, when she has had time to get the documents from the bank. Turn to 44.

160
You approach a small side-window. Roll two dice. If the result is higher than or equal to your SKILL, turn to 82. If the result is less than your SKILL, turn to 121.

161
'Now,' it cries, turning white as a sheet, 'begone!' The doors open and you are sent flying by some mysterious force into the corridor beyond. The doors slam shut. Will you continue to explore the asteroid (turn to 346), or return to Kether and either go to investigate the Customs officials (turn to 337) or search for some other clue (turn to 231)?

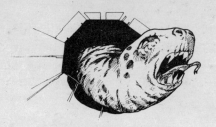

162

'Hmm,' he muses after pocketing the cash. 'I guess it's about time for my coffee break. Bye.' He strolls off, out of sight. Will you go back into hiding (turn to **357**), or assume that the guard will tell somebody of your presence? If you assume the latter, then you will have to leave the starport and search for a new clue (turn to **231**).

163

You brake just in time, for there, over the crest, is a tight hairpin bend. The sports car's six wheels squeal slightly as it whips around the corner and flies on to a long, straight downhill slope. The sloop is about 100 metres in front. Will you push the car faster (turn to **115**), or stay at your present speed (turn to **124**)?

164

The vidilink is broken and the files are just meaningless rows of numbers. You continue your desultory search through the remnants of the office for a while, but eventually give up. Turn to 203.

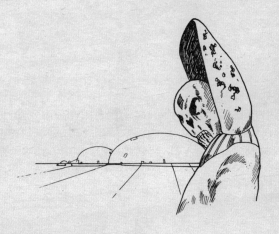

165

Zera is immobile. The vidilink is on fire; the desk is riddled with bullets. Looking around, you find nothing of note within the room. Turn to 126.

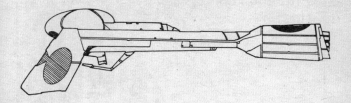

166

You enter a room which has gravity. Before you is a wide, deep pit spanned by a narrow bridge with no handrail. On the bridge stands a tripedal alien holding electric bracers in each of its three paws. It is considering you with three eyes. Thankfully, it has only one mouth, albeit a *very* large one. 'Halt,' it says, and then, without waiting to see if you do, fires several bright bolts of electrons at you. If you possess any Satophil-d, turn to **127**; otherwise turn to **88**.

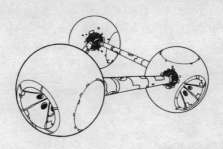

167

The terminus is largely empty, with only a few staff about. You make your way to the control sector of the building, where you find a pair of off-duty air-traffic controllers drinking some brown goop from a machine in one of the corners.

'Yech!' is the first thing they say to you. 'Oh . . . oh, that is really *horrible*,' is the second. Introducing yourself as an off-world travelling salesman, you attempt to engage them in a conversation about the lack of traffic around the port.

'Thank the stars,' says one. 'You should see it the rest of the week. Phew!'

'Busy?'

'Rather.'

Upon your bringing up the subject of unidentified helijets or illegal traffic, they look at each other, down their goop and scoot away into the restricted area of the control sector. 'Gotta go.' 'Bye-bye.' They are gone: suspicious behaviour or just a reluctance to talk shop? You could find the information from other sources, though. You can go to the City Central Library (turn to **80**) or the State Computer File Centre, which might have air-traffic records (turn to **246**); or, if you haven't already, you could approach the man working on the rental helijets (turn to **128**).

168

He looks contemptuously down his nose at you and removes his pince-nez. 'No, no. That will never do.' He must have pressed an alarm bell with his foot, because in the next moment several security guards enter the room and grapple with you. Turn to **129**.

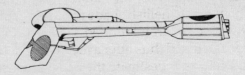

169

He looks suitably frightened. 'It's the Customs officer, he makes me do it! Don't send me to jail, please . . . please . . .' he pleads. You slap him in the face.

'Makes you do what? Come on, you're in very big trouble, mister.'

'He makes me destroy the records for certain flights . . .'

'Which flights?' you snap.

'From . . . from the islands.'

'Which island in particular?' you ask, simulating rage and pounding him against the wall.

'I . . . I don't know,' he cries. 'We only pick them up just before they . . . they reach the coast.' He collapses into a snivelling heap.

Will you really start slapping him around to see if he's hiding anything (turn to **130**), or ease off a little to show him you're human (turn to **72**)?

170

They lead you into the manor-house. Turn to **151**.

171

You float gently to the floor and move towards the pedestal. In response, the flame leaps to the ceiling and changes to a hellish shade of purple. You notice that two heavy, iron-studded wooden doors in a wall are open and thus offer a means of exit from the room. Will you investigate the pedestal closer (turn to **83**), or leave via the open doors (turn to **132**)?

172

Slowly, you open the locker door, slide out and creep towards an aisle between the next row of lockers. Roll two dice. If the result is higher than or equal to your SKILL, turn to **133**. If the result is less than your SKILL, turn to **123**.

173

You enter the forest at 240 k.p.h., only to find the road curving in tight S-bends between thick clumps of trees. You fight with the steering-wheel to keep the car under control. *Test your Luck.* If you are successful, turn to **134**; otherwise turn to **270**.

174

You hit them just above the rear mudguard, fortuitously locking one of the back wheels, stripping a differential and sending the massive black car through the guard-rail and rolling down the embankment. It flips, smashes and is still – certainly a fatal crash. You pull over to the side of the road. Turn to **359**.

175

'Scorpion,' you answer. The machine does not even bother to tell you that you were wrong before opening fire on you. Turn to **97**.

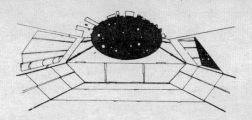

176

You struggle free. With snapping teeth and writhing tentacles, it pursues you back to the tunnel, but follows no further. You decide to try jumping from sphere to sphere. Turn to **137**.

177

Having defeated your foe, you might as well find out why he was attacking you. A search of his body reveals little, though; there is his rifle, a small mechanical component and a ticket, via Pan-Kether Spaceways, from Rispin's End to Kether.

The mechanical component, under close examination, reveals itself to be a pressure bearing from a helijet. Perhaps his normal job, when he wasn't killing people, was a jet mechanic. You look at his hands: short nails with grease under them – could be from cleaning his rifle, though.

The ticket to Kether is made out for a B. Smith, stated occupation librarian. There doesn't seem to be much point in staying on the moon, so you return to Kether. You can either go out to one of the heliports around the capital (turn to **206**), or perhaps do a bit of research at the library (turn to **80**).

178

The large sliding door is unlocked and pushes open easily, revealing a quite dark interior; the shadowy outlines of crates and, in front of you, a ground car are barely defined. Quietly and carefully, you creep inside. Suddenly, six or seven men jump out from behind the crates with blasters pointing at you. One of them yells, '*Stop!*' Will you freeze where you are (turn to **100**), or take a gamble and dive for cover (turn to **139**)?

179

They are unlocked and contain mainly junk – mainly, but not completely, for there, under a pile of bent paperclips and rusting staples, is a 'gem'. It is a letter from the Head Customs Officer to the Air-traffic Chief:

> *Dear Aestho,*
> *Here's your cheque. Note that today's flight from the east coast – No. 212 – was 'unusual' and should be written off as per the others. Contents will be cleared tomorrow, so tomorrow's shuttle to Tau Ceti – No. 005 – should also be written off.*
>
> *Zac Kalensus*

The cheque is for 3,000 kopecks! Will you pay a visit to Customs (turn to **337**), or try to find someone in the space industry who might know about the illegal traffic (to Tau Ceti, for instance) hinted at in the letter (turn to **384**)?

180

Test your Luck. If you are successful, turn to **102**; otherwise turn to **141**.

181

He caches the extra 2,000 away in a shirt pocket and signals you closer. 'Top floor of the Isosceles Tower, in the city,' he whispers. 'That's their nerve centre.' He then mumbles something about being out of a job and rushes back into the freight depot, out of sight. You could check out this tip by going to the Isosceles Tower (turn to **320**), or follow up his first clue by looking for the satellite (turn to **36**).

182

You are not far from your goal, but in a slow spin, so the white vapour from the jets tumbles at an odd angle. If you're not careful you'll miss the satellite completely. Roll two dice. If the result is higher than or equal to your SKILL, turn to **104**. If the result is less than your SKILL, turn to **143**.

183

You misplaced your bumper on the side of the other vehicle. The collision sends your car sideways, off the road and sailing into a tree at 160 k.p.h. You have failed.

184

It is an Androform, constructed in the shape of a fierce hound. You will have to fight the machine hand to hand.

ANDROFORM   SKILL 9   STAMINA 8

If you defeat it, turn to 145.

185

The exit leads you down another zero-gravity tunnel to a crossroads. You have three tunnels to choose from.

Straight ahead	Turn to 293
Left	Turn to 332
Right	Turn to 146

186

Which door button will you press:

Front?	Turn to 79
Back?	Turn to 40
Left?	Turn to 381
Right?	Turn to 342
Up?	Turn to 303
Down?	Turn to 264

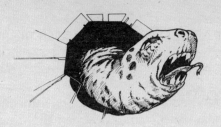

187

You give chase but, for all her fat and age, the woman is amazingly fleet of foot – you lose sight of her down a side-street. Luck is on your side in one way, however. In her rush to escape, she dropped her bag, which contains 500 kopecks and a small number of business cards, all of which read:

Z. GROSS
STELLAR AND INTERPLANETARY
IMPORT/EXPORT

Strangely, there is no vidinumber or address. Still, it's something to go on. You return to your ship and decide, the next day, to go to the City Central Library to see if there is anything to find out concerning this Z. Gross. Turn to **80**.

188

Circling around towards the back of the hangar-sized warehouse, you discover a small door partly hidden behind some piles of rubbish. You force this entrance rather easily. In front of you is a short corridor which ends in two doors, indistinguishable from each other. You approach the doors. Which will you go through: the left (**149**) or the right (**3**)?

189

In the city you find a few interstellar and interplanetary shipping agencies to ask some questions of – all of which give unsatisfactory replies. While you are in a sandwich bar, picking up some lunch between agencies, you are confronted by two men – each holding a blaster no more than fifteen centimetres from your belly. 'Come with us,' they say, 'or we will kill you.' You'd have no chance of escape at this distance. You go with them out the back of the shop. Turn to **316**.

190

The conduit heads further into the asteroid until you find your way blocked by an enormous maintenance and pest-killing robot. Its three eyes swivel to watch you approach. It flicks a tentative laser blast at you to see if you fall into the 'pest' category that it holds in its machine mind. There's no way past, even if you destroyed it, and, as it begins to lumber towards you, it may even pose a threat. You return to the grille overlooking the room, push it open and enter. Turn to **171**.

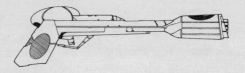

191

You run out on to the road, narrowly being missed by a carload of picnickers – out for a jolly time in the gardens. The black sloop is tearing down the street, past another car which is heading toward you. Will you shoot at the villains' car (turn to **152**), or try to flag the other car down so as to give chase (turn to **113**)?

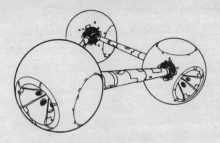

192
You rocket into a high orbit around Kether. *Test your Luck*. If you are successful, turn to **153**; otherwise turn to **114**.

193
You slide along the shoulders, but retain a grip on the road with the other three wheels. The car slingshots out of the S-bend at a terrific pace and ends up only three metres behind the sloop. Turn to **378**.

194
Turn to **116**.

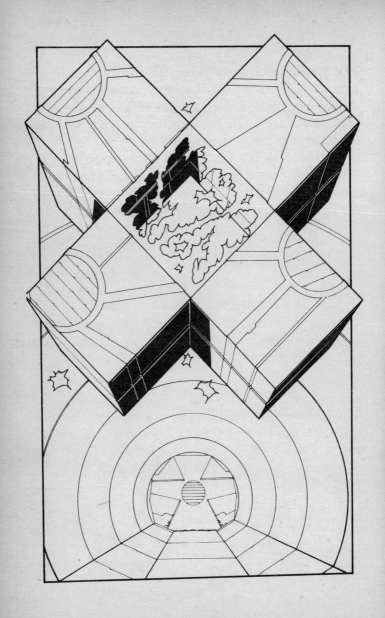

195

The tunnel ends in a large cylindrical chamber. Floating in front of you, blocking your passage, is a device constructed of four cubes set in the shape of an X with a cubic hole in the centre. Bright blue bolts of electricity fly between the cubes through the central hole. With a low hum, it begins to approach. The flashing becomes more frequent and begins to lash out towards you in great electric arcs. Will you fire at this device with your blaster (turn to 78), try to dive past it (turn to 39), or take a flying leap at it to hit it with your boots and thus (hopefully) send it out of control (turn to 380)?

196

You receive an electric shock from the door. It does not open. Lose 1 point of STAMINA and then return to 225.

197

You run down the stairwell, but by the time you reach ground level and launch yourself into the street the man is nowhere to be seen. You have lost him. Suddenly, a scream comes from above you: *'Murder!'* Just what you need. Within seconds, proctor helijets descend from the sky, landing in the street and on the hotel's roof. Another helijet, hovering between the surrounding buildings, fixes a room on the twelfth floor – most certainly 1201 – with a spotlight. Proctors, procs, cops – call them what you will – seem to be everywhere.

Not knowing if the local procs can be trusted, you decide to lie low. Next day, you head off to the City Central Library to see if anything can be found out about the man you saw running down the stairs – at least you know what he looks like. Turn to **80**.

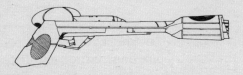

198

'Good-day, Mrs Torus, I am an Investigator from Federal Central (Vice). Could I have a word with your husband?' you ask in your most official voice. She looks up and down the street and then ushers you in.

199

'Clive . . . Clive's dead,' she cries, bursting into tears. 'They killed him!'

'Who, Mrs Torus, who?'

'His mates, the people he worked with. He didn't want to work for them any more so . . . so they killed him.'

You discover from her that her husband took care of a lot of the accounts for Zera Gross (his boss, evidently), and that these accounts were kept by Clive in a safety-deposit box at one of the banks in the city. They are still there. 'I . . . I can get them for you, if you like,' she says.

'Yes, that would be very useful, thank you.' Clive may have kept other incriminating documents around the house – perhaps you should ask his wife if you could look through his personal papers? She looks very upset though. Will you ask her (turn to **120**) or not (turn to **159**)?

199

Circling through the trees, you let the sounds of pursuit pass you – heading for the security fence, no doubt. Before you is the house, a rambling two-storey structure in the style of Neo-starquest Colonial. Quite tasteless, really. As it is becoming fairly dark, you could try climbing on to the roof to look for a way in (turn to **43**), or simply force a ground-floor window or door (turn to **160**).

200

'Now,' it cries, turning as white as a sheet, 'begone!' The doors open and you are sent flying by some mysterious force into the corridor beyond. The doors slam shut. Will you continue to explore the asteroid (turn to 346), or assume that you're in the wrong part of space and head back to Kether (turn to 231)?

201

Turn to 162.

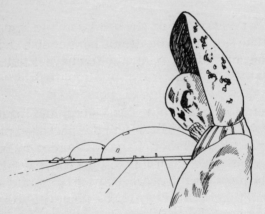

202

The sloop flies down the straight and disappears over a hump-backed hill. You cannot see what happens to the road past the crest. Will you assume that the road continues straight and take the crest at high speed (turn to 309), or will you anticipate a corner and slow down a bit (turn to 163)?

203

There is another door at the other end of the office. You go through it, down a short corridor and then through yet another door. Turn to **86**.

204

Using her massive bulk, she beats you into insensibility. The last thing you hear is her fiendish cackle and 'Har, har. Stupid narc . . .' You have failed.

205

The corridor leads to a small storeroom where, evidently, the finished Satophil-d is packaged prior to shipment to Kether. Large quantities in both powder and tablet form are present. You may take a small amount as evidence if you wish. If so, add it to your Equipment List. Leaving the store, you go back into the laboratory and through the other exit. Turn to **166**.

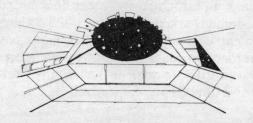

206

You take a cab out to the heliport on the city outskirts. It is a large desolate slab of concrete under a harsh sun with a few low buildings rising at what you suppose is the terminus. Nothing moves. There are a couple of rental helijets grouped by a hut and a few service vehicles parked next to the terminus. A man comes out of the hut and proceeds to work on one of the helijets, opening its turbines for inspection. You could either direct a few questions at this man from the rental company (turn to 128), or go to the terminus (turn to 167).

207

You approach the receptionist, a seemingly pleasant fellow with pince-nez. 'I'd like to look at a few files, if I may?' 'Oh, yes,' he says, greedily rubbing his hands together. 'What century would you like, hmmm!' 'Oh, this century, just the last few years, actually,' you say, nonchalantly. He begins to bob up and down in agitation. 'Ah, no. I'm afraid we can't let you see them . . .' Will you now hold out 1,000 kopecks under his nose (turn to 168) or 2,000 (turn to 373)?

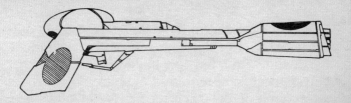

208

You withdraw your blaster from its holster, stick the barrel in his face and push him around. He slams against a wall and slides to the floor. 'I am a Federal Narcotics Investigator and I hear, Mr Air-traffic Controller, that you've got something to hide. Out with it! Everything you know,' you say in an icy voice. *Test your Luck*. If you are successful, turn to **169**; otherwise turn to **33**.

209

One of the gunmen, although off balance, manages to trip you up with a kick to your shins. You fall. 'I wouldn't try that again, sunshine,' says a scar-faced thug, sticking the barrel of his gun in your ear. They rough you up a bit before dragging you to your feet. Turn to **170**.

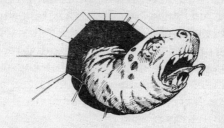

210

You see, too late, that she is dead. The sloop has disappeared from view. Looks like you need a new clue now. Turn to 231.

211

The freight depot is quite enormous, but you find a row of lockers in which you can hide and still get a good view of any comings and goings. You share a locker with a couple of greatcoats and a pin-up – the depot can be seen through a few ventilation slots. After a short while, you notice, to your dismay, a khaki-clad security officer, armed with a gigantic blaster, checking your row of lockers. He opens each one in turn, slowly approaching the one you are hiding in. Will you try to move from your locker without being seen (turn to 172), or stay where you are, hide behind a coat and hope he doesn't find you (turn to 84)?

212

The road and sloop disappear into a wood, 300 metres ahead. There is no telling what happens to the road in there. Will you accelerate to catch up (turn to **173**), or stay at the same speed (turn to **46**)?

213

Unfortunately, the sloop is bigger and heavier than your vehicle and your inexpert side-swipe leaves you open to retaliation of a like kind. The behemoth bears down on you, smashing your car out of control and through the guard-rail. Your car rolls violently down the embankment, stopping at the bottom to explode. You have failed.

214

'Antares,' you answer. The machine lowers itself to the floor and says, just before shutting itself down, 'Correct. Pass.' Turn to **58**.

215

You cannot break free, and the monster sets its teeth in you. You have failed.

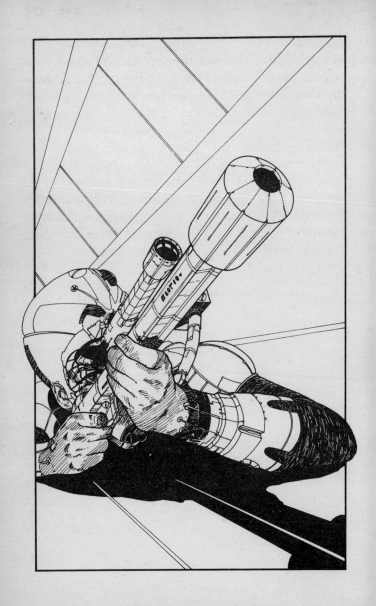

216

You take cover behind the scooter and draw your pistol. The assassin is lying on the ground firing a high-powered rifle.

ASSASSIN   SKILL 8   STAMINA 6

If you defeat him, turn to 177.

217

You enter the warehouse grounds. Will you enter the building via the large main entrance at the front (turn to 178), or have a look around the outside first (turn to 188)?

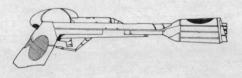

218

The office is empty, bar the usual equipment and furniture. You probably won't have very long, so will you search on the vidi in the room for his private computer files (turn to 140), or go through his desk drawers instead (turn to 179)?

219

The ramp leads, perhaps fortuitously, to a balcony overlooking the great hall. It is packed with a throng of black-robed figures. They begin to chant and sway. A couple of men out in front swing burning incense in great circles. Soon, a man, obviously the MC, high priest or such, appears out in front and begins a long prayer to some holy malevolence known as Thuvald. Obviously, you have the wrong place – this is a monastery, a weird one no doubt, but still a monastery. You sneak out of the balcony, away from C230 and head back to Kether. Turn to 231.

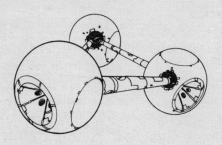

220

'Fine,' he says, taking the money. 'What do you want to know?'

'Drugs,' you say. 'Where do they come from, and who do they go to?' He looks a bit uneasy about this topic. 'Well, I . . . I don't know much about that, but I think it's got something to do with a satellite in an L16 orbit. Irregular transmissions . . . you might try looking for it . . .'

'Transmissions to whom?' you ask.

He rubs his fingers together. 'For another 2,000 kopecks I *might* be able to help you,' he says.

Will you pay him another 2,000 (turn to **181**), or give up on him and find another Customs official, but this time try a bit of rough stuff (turn to **142**)? Alternatively, you could look for the satellite that he mentioned (turn to **36**).

221

You reach the satellite safely and attach a magnetic clamp to it, to prevent you from drifting away into space. You remove a communications cable from your pack, open a service panel on the side of the satellite and attach the cable to a diagnostic inlet on the satellite's computer. Now you can determine its function, where it receives its transmissions from and where it sends them on to.

Returning to your ship, you find that the satellite receives from an unknown asteroid and transmits to the top floor of the Isosceles Tower in the centre of Kether's capital. The messages are all concerned with shipments of the drug Satophil-d from the asteroid to the planet. Pity you don't know where this asteroid is, but you do know where the Isosceles Tower is. You return to Kether. Turn to **320**.

222

You scrape bumpers with it and plant your foot as you hit a curve. Roll two dice. If the result is higher than or equal to your SKILL, turn to **183**. If the result is less than your SKILL, turn to **144**.

223

'Nice dog, hey? Who's a nice dog?' you simper, while holding out a hand to it. It slavers, opens its massive maw, and bites your arm. Lose 1 point of SKILL. Turn to **184**.

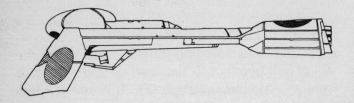

224

You misjudge badly, and the sentinel reacts sharply by moving in such a way that you fly through the hole in the centre of the four cubes. While you are doing this it covers the hole with sheets of lightning. You are fried.

225

Which door button will you press:

Front?	Turn to 118
Back?	Turn to 157
Left?	Turn to 196
Right?	Turn to 235
Down?	Turn to 274
Up?	Turn to 313

226

As you jump from behind a ground car into a shadow by a building, you trip over a small motor unicycle left in the middle of the sidewalk. There is a tremendous crash as it falls over. The woman, looking round, sees you. She starts running down the street. Roll two dice. If the result is higher than or equal to your SKILL, turn to 187. If the result is less than your SKILL, turn to 148.

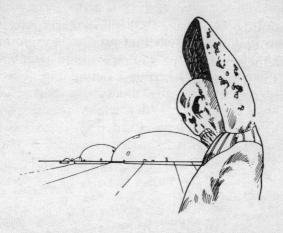

227

Cautiously, you approach him. 'I'm Clive Torus. We may be able to do some business together,' he says rather furtively. 'Oh yes? How?' you reply, warily. 'Meet me at the Café Heroes of the Federation at nine o'clock, tomorrow morning. We'll talk there.' He then turns and scuttles off into the bowels of the warehouse.

You could meet him tomorrow (turn to 315), or, knowing that the thugs are expecting a shipment from the asteroids that evening, you could try to find somebody in the space industry who may know something about illegal space traffic (turn to 384).

228

'Illegal space traffic?' he muses, turning a few switches on the panel in front of him. 'Yes, a bit of that goes on around here . . . so I'm told.' You press him to be more specific. 'Well,' he says, looking around to make certain that no one is listening, 'there's this asteroid – C230 – out in the main belt, which has a lot of suspicious comings and goings. You might try there – the co-ordinates for it would be in any Cosmo-Nav.' Will you take his advice and have a look at this asteroid (turn to 73), or go back to the city to try to verify his information (turn to 189)?

229

The vent leads through some machinery, a couple of automatic airlocks and, eventually, into some air-conditioning conduits. The occupants of the asteroid don't seem to possess any gravity generators, and you float through the air-conditioning until you come to an outlet. Looking through the grille you can see a large rough-hewn room. It is very dim – the only light comes from a guttering red flame burning on a pedestal in the centre of the room. Will you push out the grille and enter the room (turn to **171**), or continue through the air-conditioning (turn to **190**)?

230

If you are willing to part with at least 2,000 kopecks, you can try to bribe a Customs officer for information (turn to **298**); otherwise you will have to resort to a bit of rough stuff on one of them (turn to **142**).

231

You have very little to go on really, almost no options at all. Will you:

Return to Kether's capital city to have a look around?	Turn to **75**
Search in space for a new clue?	Turn to **192**
Search for C230, assuming you have heard of it and have not already sought it out?	Turn to **73**

232

You lose control, and slide off the road and across country for a short distance. The car comes to rest in a boggy paddock. Your windshield is covered with mud, badly restricting your visibility. The windshield wipers can hardly move the stuff so, while you are driving the car, reduce your SKILL by 1. With wheels spinning, you drive across the slippery field and back on to the road. Turn to **387**.

233

Turn to **116**.

234

Behind the door is a room full of pressure-suits and emergency air-tents. There is nothing of use inside the asteroid – only out of it. You leave the room and go back down the tunnel. Turn to **195**.

235

You receive an electric shock from the door. It does not open. Lose 1 point of STAMINA and then return to **225**.

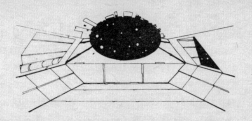

236

You tap gently on the door. No answer. You tap again. A groan comes from within. You try the door, but it is locked. The seconds are ticking away. The ever more distant sound of steps going down can still be heard. Will you force your way into the room (turn to **158**), or go in pursuit of the man who just went down the stairs (turn to **197**)?

237

'I'm one of Clive's . . . er . . . colleagues,' you say. 'Do you know where he is?' Her face twists and she begins to cry. 'Oh, why don't you leave us alone – go back to Spark's where all your filthy mates hang out . . .' and then slams the door in your face.

Well, well. 'Spark's', you discover, is a bar down by the starport. Might as well go and have a look there. Turn to **286**.

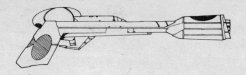

238

The gunmen are taken by surprise; by the time they start shouting, you are sprinting across a mini astro-turf golf course towards a copse of trees. There you pause: behind you are shots and shouts; in front, nothing bar the security fence. You could escape the manor-house environs, although the drug runners are certain to abandon the manor once they discover you have fled, so you will have to look for a new clue (turn to **231**), or you could double back to the house, break in and find out what's going on (turn to **199**).

239

It flaps its great wings to stand upright, considers you with unnerving malice, and speaks:

'In the wrong place, you are.
Misled, you have been.
With the Customs officials, you should be.'

Turn to **161**.

240

Turn to **162**.

241

Taking the access road cuts the distance between the sloop and your car to a mere 100 metres. You rejoin the main road just as it straightens. Turn to **202**.

242

You pick a few files from the floor and seat yourself behind a computer vidilink. Roll two dice. If the result is higher than or equal to your SKILL, turn to **164**. If the result is less than your SKILL, turn to **125**.

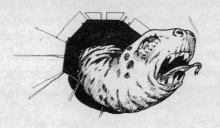

243

She lies, whale-like, immobile and exhausted. 'Zera,' you say, slapping her face, 'tell me about the organization.' Unfortunately, she is extremely dazed and can only mumble, 'Up . . . up, then left . . .' Turn to **126**.

244

You make it to the third sphere. From here you easily make it to the other exit. Turn to **283**.

245

Crouched low over his beer, as if he is trying to hide his head in his shoulders, he begins to mutter a long, paranoid tale about the Tau Cygni threat (whatever that is). Due to the noise in the bar, and the navigator's dull voice, you miss most of his monologue and find, when he suddenly and unexpectedly reaches the end of his tale, that the only information you have gleaned from him is his suspicion that something odd is going on at Rispin's End and that the fat broad playing cards at the table behind you has something to do with it. What to make of that? Will you go out to Rispin's End (the moon) to see if anything is to be found (turn to 398), or will you keep an eye on the woman at the table behind you (turn to 343)?

246

The State Computer File Centre is a squat, ugly rectangle of concrete surrounded by a few kilometres of razor wire. A large metal sign, wired to one of the fences, flaps lazily in the wind: TRESPASSERS PROSECUTED. There is, however, a public entrance into a tiny pillbox set away from the main building. You enter this building and notice, to your dismay, yet another large sign:

ONLY THOSE FILES WHICH ARE MORE THAN 100 YEARS OLD WILL BE RELEASED FOR PUBLIC PERUSAL

It seems that you are going to have to resort to a felony to get the information you want. Will you try bribery (turn to 207), or breaking and entering (turn to 90)?

247

At the heliport there is a large display of holographs headed with the slogan:

WE HAVE *YOUR* COMFORT AND SAFETY IN MIND

The holographs are of all the staff involved in the running of the port. There are, you notice, two chiefs of air traffic – you make note of what their smiling countenances look like, hire a ground car, and wait in the staff car-park. After a few hours one of the chiefs emerges from the port, climbs into a ground car and drives off. You follow him home. When you approach him, will you act tough to extract the necessary information (turn to **208**), or will you act friendly (turn to **296**)?

248

Presently a couple of gunmen appear at the end of the corridor. They call for you to surrender. You take a few potshots at them to demonstrate your resolve. In response, they throw a small device down at you. It explodes into a cloud of clinging vapour. A gas bomb! You try not to breathe but still you begin to lose consciousness. Obviously, it is nerve gas, entering your system through the tear ducts in your eyes. You black out. When you come to, you discover that you are being supported on either side by a burly thug. Turn to **151**.

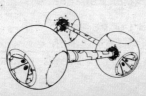

249

With one shot the sniper is sent plummeting to the ground, dead. Reholstering your gun, you walk to meet Mrs Torus. 'Good day, Mrs Torus,' you say. 'Have you the documents?' 'Yes, they're right here,' she says, showing you the safety-deposit box. 'Goo . . .' There is an explosion at your very feet. Somebody planted a bomb! Everything is thrown in the air. One of the glasshouses collapses. Throw two dice and deduct the total from your STAMINA. If you survive, continue.

You rise groggily to your knees, just in time to see, over the still form of Mrs Torus, a slick young man climbing into the ground sloop you saw parked behind the glasshouse. He is carrying the box of documents. The sloop drives off. Will you try to chase the car (turn to 191), or let them go and tender aid to Mrs Torus (turn to 210)?

250

The dome-covered base has a population of about 300. You don't detect anything even remotely suspicious there – a few tourists and lots of scientists and technicians. You hire a small rocket scooter for a few days, to scour the surface of this tiny moon (deduct 500 kopecks to cover costs). The search, however, proves fruitless: you find a couple of prospectors and one technical team looking at vacuum welding of the moon's crust, but no illegal drug manufacturers. You leave Rispin's End and head for the main planet, Kether. Turn to 333.

251

Sliding out on to the verge, you manage to keep the car under control. You change down, accelerate and slingshot down a long gentle slope. The sloop is still far ahead, doing a good 190 k.p.h. Will you accelerate to catch it (turn to 124), or play safe and just match its speed (turn to 212)?

252

A quick twist of the steering-wheel sends your sports car careering into the side of the large black sloop. Paint strips, metal shrieks and sparks fly. Roll two dice. If the result is higher than or equal to your SKILL, turn to **213**. If the result is less than your SKILL, turn to **174**.

253

The corridor leads you to an octagonal room. Standing in the centre, contemplating you with at least four of its seven electronic sensors, is a chrome and silver robot, obviously of alien design and manufacture. 'Welcome,' it sighs, rising up on its seven articulated legs and extending a few antennae and microwave sensors in your direction. Then it continues:

'Red I am,
the heart of a scorpion,
yet not of Arachnia at all!
Pincers I have,
but I grasp with the unseen.
In one word, what am I?'

With which letter of the alphabet does the answer begin:

A?	Turn to **214**
S?	Turn to **175**
X?	Turn to **136**

254

Sticking close to the walls of the cavern, you float towards the other side. One of the creatures brushes you with a tentacle, then another, and another. Suddenly, it wraps half a dozen around you and drags you from the wall. What's worse, you discover that these creatures are almost entirely teeth. It tries to eat you. Roll two dice. If the result is higher than or equal to your SKILL, turn to **215**. If the result is less than your SKILL, turn to **176**.

255

Taking a helicab to Proctor HQ (the local police are known as proctors) gives you a good idea of the size of Kether's capital – in fact, its only city. A burgeoning little metropolis about ten kilometres in diameter, with a few quaint fifty-storey office blocks and apartment towers for a city centre. Lots of helijets; lots of ground cars; no peds. A normal fringe capital really. You arrive at Proctor HQ in the city centre and make your way from the fiftieth storey of the tower to the forty-ninth, where Vice is located.

'Excuse me,' you say to the duty proctor at the reception. 'I would like to speak to one of the senior investigators.'

'Oh . . .' says the ageing and sleepy man. 'Er . . . yes, right this way.'

Throw a die. If the result is even, turn to **96**; otherwise turn to **297**.

256

The place, when you find it on the city outskirts, turns out to be a large, run-down warehouse. Turn to **217**.

257

A quick search of the directory in the foyer of the port administration block reveals the location of the Air-traffic Chief's office. You knock on his door, but there is no reply. Quietly, you open it and step in. Throw a die. If the result is even, turn to **218**; if odd, turn to **23**.

258

Somewhere, a gong sounds. The deep resonance booming through the asteroid causes the very rocks to vibrate. The two men bow their heads in response and float off down another corridor. After a moment you follow them, coming eventually to a nexus. More black-robed figures are pouring out of other corridors and into a great hall – seems to be quite a gathering. Will you try to slip into the hall unnoticed after the last men enter (turn to **180**), or take a ramp next to the hall (turn to **219**)?

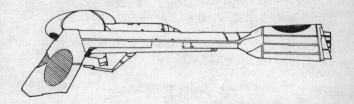

259

'Fine,' he says, taking the money. 'What do you want to know?'

'Drugs,' you say. 'Where do they come from, and who do they go to?'

He looks a bit uneasy about this topic. 'Well, I . . . I don't know much about that, but I think it's got something to do with a satellite in an L16 orbit. Irregular transmissions . . . you might try looking for it . . .'

'Transmissions to whom?' you ask.

'I . . . I can't say.' He turns suddenly and runs back into the freight depot. Well, you could go and look for this satellite (turn to 36), or find another Customs official, but this time try a bit of rough stuff (turn to 142).

260

White vapour bursts from the jets, which carry you at a slow drift towards the satellite. You seem to have made it about half-way, but you will have to use your jets again to adjust your course, otherwise you are likely just to miss landing on the satellite. You fire the jets again. Roll two dice. If the result is higher than or equal to your SKILL, turn to 182. If the result is less than your SKILL, turn to 221.

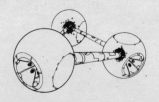

261
Taking the side-road reduces the distance between your two cars to a few metres. You come out behind them just as they finish the curve. Turn to 378.

262
You draw your blaster as the beast leaps, slavering, at your throat. Turn to 184.

263
The sentinel spins out of control and dashes itself to pieces against the walls of the chamber. When it has finally stopped sparking, you move past it, towards the exit. Turn to 185.

264
A short blade flicks from the button and slashes your hand. The door does not open. Lose 1 point of SKILL. Return to 186.

265

After a few hours, the woman surges to her feet with an enormous burp and staggers from the bar into the street. The men she was playing with, now looking dishevelled and tired, lay down their cards and order drinks from the bar. It seems they are going to stay for a while longer. You put down your glass and slip after the woman. It is dark outside, thus affording you plenty of concealment as you follow her. Roll two dice. If the result is higher than or equal to your SKILL, turn to 226. If the result is less than your SKILL, turn to 70.

266

You scuttle along the gantry, away from the man and out of the warehouse. The only worthwhile clue you have left is the knowledge that the thugs' 'shipment' was coming from the asteroids. You decide to find somebody in the space industry who may know something about illegal space traffic. Turn to 384.

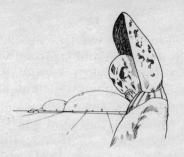

267

He agrees to talk to you for 500 kopecks – subtract this sum from your credit account. Turn to 228.

268

You sit at his feet. 'I think, sir,' he begins, 'that you have been misinformed about certain things – in short, led astray.' 'Oh?' you say. 'Yes. This asteroid is a monastery. Nothing more, nothing illegal. I suggest, when you get back to Kether, that you pay a visit to the Customs officials at the starport – well, goodbye.' He waves his hands and shouts something unintelligible at you. Instantly, you find yourself back aboard your spacecraft. You start back for Kether. Will you take the Grand Keeper's advice and visit Customs (turn to 337), or try to find another clue instead (turn to 231)?

269

You climb on to the roof of the passenger terminal, find a maintenance duct, and crawl into the ceiling. Eventually, you find your way through all the wiring, automatic fire-extinguishers and anti-terrorist gear to a position just above the Customs' check-in point. You wait, and wait, and wait. Nobody arrives. Nothing happens. Obviously, the passenger terminal is no hotbed of crime and vice. It's too late to go and hide in the freight depot, but you'll still have time to get out of the ceiling and approach a Customs official (turn to 230). Alternatively, you can forget about the starport and carry your inquiries elsewhere (turn to 231).

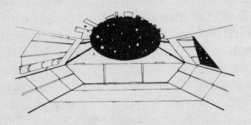

270

The car goes out of control, slides from the road and rolls violently across the ground. Eventually it is stopped by a tree – a total wreck. It explodes. You have failed.

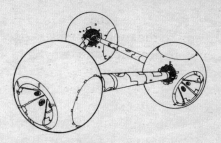

271

The shoulders *are* soft and give way under your car. Roll two dice. If the result is higher than or equal to your SKILL, turn to **232**. If the result is less than your SKILL, turn to **193**.

272

You say the first thing that springs to mind: 'Wrench?' The machine hums a bit and floats into a recess in the ceiling: 'Pass.' Turn to **77**.

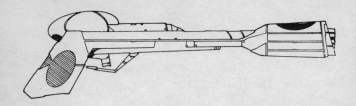

273

The surface of the asteroid is pock-marked and glowing from your assault. You bring your spacecraft down and space-walk across to the airlock. Once through it, you find yourself at the end of a long zero-gravity tunnel, heading into the bowels of the asteroid. Floating down it, you come across an airtight security door set in one of the walls. It is unmarked. Will you continue down the tunnel (turn to **195**), or go through the door (turn to **234**)?

274

You receive an electric shock from the door. It does not open. Lose 1 point of STAMINA and then return to **225**.

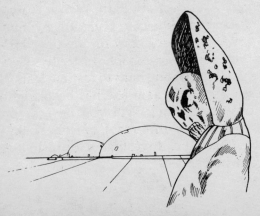

275

At the dome town, you decide to hire a small rocket scooter for a few days (deduct 500 kopecks to cover costs). When you return to your pressure-suit and scooter after paying for the hire, you find that somebody has slipped a note into your helmet. It reads: *If you want to grow old, leave Aleph Cygni.*

Cute. There doesn't seem to be anyone around who could have slipped it in – must've got away quickly. You spend a few days going over the surface of Rispin's End but, apart from a few small mining outposts, find absolutely nothing to indicate the presence of any illicit activity. You return to the dome town. After you park your scooter, a shot rings out from behind a giant garbage compactor, the bullet ricocheting off the ground in front of you. An assassin! Will you return the fire (turn to **216**), or try to get away (turn to **138**)?

276

You look him up in the vidiphone directory. There is only one C. Torus, of 113 Fifth Avenue, City. You catch a helicab into the city, find Fifth Avenue and Torus's apartment. A knock on the door brings a woman in answer – probably his wife. 'He's not here,' she says, fighting hard to restrain tears. 'He's not here.' She looks as if she has been frightfully upset over something. Will you pose as one of Clive's colleagues (turn to **237**), or let her know that you are a Narcotics Investigator (turn to **198**), to elicit his whereabouts?

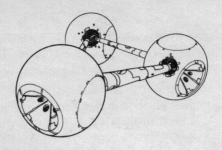

277

You dive for the privet hedge! *Test your Luck*. If you are successful, turn to **238**; otherwise turn to **209**.

278

It flaps its great wings to stand upright and considers you with unnerving malice. 'You are in a most holy spot,' it hisses between steel teeth. 'A monastery dedicated to the merciless Thuvald of Kyth.' Turn to **200**.

279

Turn to **162**.

280

To stay on the road, you have to brake drastically. However, you make it safely through. Turn to **387**.

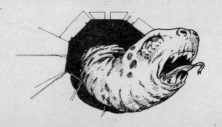

281

The antigrav dray is a massive grey device, about the size of two helijets put end to end. It floats a metre off the ground. You could attempt to drive it into and through the freight door to give whatever might be waiting behind it a nasty shock (turn to 292), or, if this doesn't appeal, you could leave the dray and enter, on foot, one of the lesser entrances (turn to 311 or 301), or the freight entrance (turn to 67).

282

You jump over the desk at her, and send both of you sprawling on the floor. You trade punches in hand-to-hand combat.

ZERA GROSS   SKILL 8   STAMINA 11

If you defeat her, turn to 243; otherwise turn to 204.

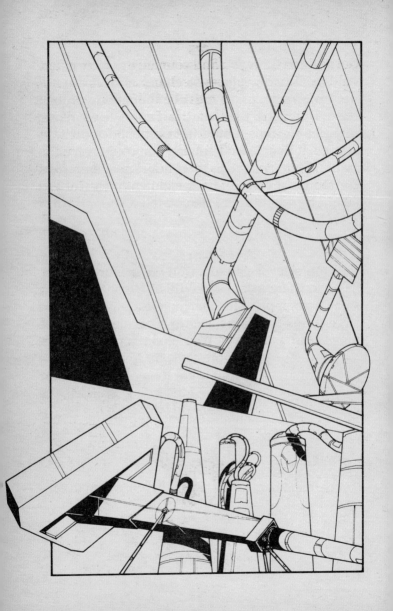

283

Going through it, you find yourself in a large chemical laboratory; stainless-steel and glass apparatus rise on all sides. This must be the factory proper. Here is where most of the Federation's illegal Satophil-d comes from. There is nobody about, so you busy yourself destroying some of the equipment. While doing this, you notice two exits from the room – a door and a corridor. Which will you take? The door (turn to **166**), or the corridor (turn to **205**)?

284

Mr Samuel leads you to a grotty spaceport canteen. 'He's in there – looks like this.' He shows you a small holograph of the man in question – tall, dark, large nose – you'll be able to recognize him. 'Tell him I sent you. Bye.' You shake hands. Samuel leaves and you enter the canteen. Inside is chaos – noise, fumes and fights – but there, leaning on the bar, is your man. After identifying yourself, he leads you to an empty table to talk. Turn to **245**.

285

The statistics on transport are almost completely useless, apart from being long, tedious and very dry reading. However, you do notice that, in the case of air freight along one of the coasts of the continent, the amount of reported cargo received for total lift-capacity of aircraft used is *far below* what it should be in reference to the other coasts. Even the amount of air traffic is below normal. Perhaps there is some undeclared cargo? You leave the library and head for the State Computer File Centre in order to get a first-hand look at the files used in compiling these statistics. Turn to **246**.

286

Entering the place, you are struck by the noise and thick atmosphere – what a joint! You saunter up to the bar, order a drink and then turn to survey the crowd. Standing in front of you, blasters pointing at your stomach from fifteen centimetres away, are two men. 'Come with us,' they say matter-of-factly, 'or we will kill you.' You would almost certainly be shot to pieces if you were to try to jump them, so you do as they say. They lead you out the back. Turn to **316**.

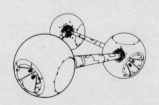

287

You creep down the corridor. An uneasy feeling begins to sneak into your mind, growing with every step. You turn and discover a security camera tracking you, the dead lens staring at your startled face. An alarm goes off, followed shortly by the sounds of feet approaching at a run. Will you make a stand (turn to 248), or escape the manor (turn to 231)?

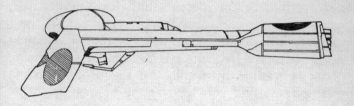

288

Drawing your blaster, you take careful aim at the sniper. Roll two dice. If the result is higher than or equal to your SKILL, turn to 74. If the result is less than your SKILL, turn to 249.

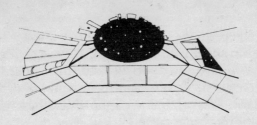

289

You orbit around Rispin's End for a few days, surveying the surface with your spy beam. There is very little to see, though – a couple of vacuum tents occupied by some prospectors, and the main base. Certainly no facility for the production of Satophil-d. Will you land at the main base for a closer inspection (turn to **250**), or give up on Rispin's End and head for Kether (turn to **333**)?

290

The black sloop is about 100 metres in front when it brakes heavily to negotiate a tight S-bend. As you approach the curves, you see that the shoulders of the road may be soft. Will you do as the sloop did, by slowing to take the S-bend (turn to **154**), or take a risk and go over the shoulders at speed (turn to **271**)?

291

The air blast from winding down your window makes it extremely difficult to aim, and the extra drag imposed on your car from this action means that the sloop begins to pull away from you. You put your gun away, wind up the window and fall back behind the sloop again. Turn to 37.

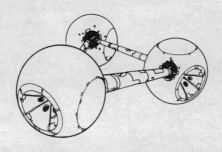

292

The drive turbines of the dray whine into life. You steer the clumsy machine towards the freight doors and push the throttle forward. It roars and accelerates at quite a frightening pace down the ramp and into the doors. They cave in. When you finally come to a rest, you find that the dray has fortuitously crushed four brutish-looking guards against the stacks of heavy-duty plastic containers they were tending. You dismount to have a look around. Turn to 28.

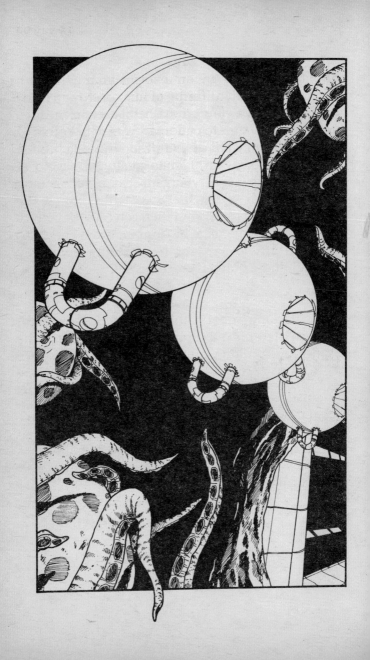

293

The tunnel ends in an enormous rough-hewn cavern. Through the centre of this cavern – in a line heading to the exit on the other side – hang three metallic spheres, each adorned with what seem to be large, loop-shaped handles. The rest of the cavern is filled with bulbous creatures, devoid of eyes or other sensory organs bar a set of long tentacles with which they constantly search the zero-gravity space around themselves. Will you try reaching the other side by jumping from sphere to sphere (turn to 137), or by wending your way through those bulbous creatures (turn to 254)?

294

The attacking robot fighters have disintegrated, their twisted remains spinning rapidly off into the void. You continue your orbital search of Rispin's End but, finding nothing, you land at the dome town to have a closer look at the surface and its inhabitants. Turn to 275.

295

You follow the man down the stairs and out into the street. He does not seem to notice you. A ground car pulls up next to him; he climbs in and is driven off. Quickly, you hail a helicab and give the immortal line, 'Follow that car!'

'Aw, come on – I don't wanna get mixed up in anything.'

'Please. It's very important,' you plead, watching the ground car slowly disappear into the traffic.

'Nah,' says the cabby. 'I don't wanna get involved. Get another cab.' You pull out your blaster and stick it in his ear. *'Follow it.'*

Reluctantly, he takes the cab into the air and pursues the car to the city outskirts where it disappears into a warehouse. You land a block away, pay the cabby and apologize for your harsh words. Turn to **217**.

296

'Excuse me, sir,' you say, pleasantly, 'I am a Federal Narcotics Investigator – I have reason to believe that you can assist me in my investigations.' His eyes glaze over and he slumps into a chair – seems to be quite terror-stricken. Turn to **33**.

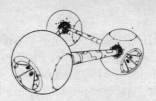

297

The proctor leads you down a long corridor, nervously doing his tie and smoothing wrinkles from his uniform. 'Normally,' he says, 'Mr Perry takes all the inquiries, but he's down the pu . . . er . . . at a meeting today, so I'll take you to see Mr Samuel instead.' He reaches Samuel's office and ushers you in.

'Hello,' you begin by way of introduction. Samuel waves the proctor from the tiny office and tells you to be seated. 'I am a Grade 1 Investigator from Federal Central (Vice). I've been sent here to crack the Aleph Cygni drug ring and would appreciate any information or aid that you might be able to give me,' you say. Mr Samuel becomes decidedly alarmed and speechless. He looks under his desk, at his desk lamp and in a potted fern; finally, he scrawls something on a piece of paper, hands it to you and pushes you from the room.

Standing in the long corridor, you read the note: *Can't speak here. Meet me at the restaurant Viqueque at 7.30 tonight*. Something is wrong, when an Investigator can't talk about crime in his own headquarters. Will you meet Mr Samuel at the restaurant Viqueque (turn to **11**), or conduct your investigations elsewhere – such as a bar or dive (turn to **299**)?

298

You approach a reedy-looking Customs official standing behind a counter in the freight reception wing. 'Psst, hey, psst, buddy,' you say by way of introducing yourself. 'I need some information.' You wave a wad of notes under his nose. He looks to see if anybody is watching and then, leaning forward over the counter, whispers, 'How much?' and points at the cash. How much will you offer him: 2,000 kopecks (turn to **259**), or 3,000 kopecks (turn to **220**)?

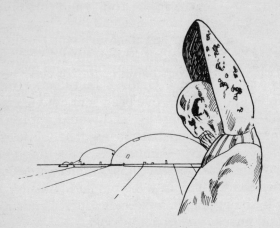

299

The canteen you find is advertised by a gaudy crypto-fluorescent animated sign, depicting a large 'Crush' class stellar battleship diving into a foaming glass of undefined liquid. The sound-effects are deafening, full of fusion-motor roars, laser zaps and dam-sized splashes. Looks promising.

Entering the premises, you find the joint packed with drunken flotsam and jetsam; there is hearty laughter, the obligatory fight in the corner and it is all very, very noisy. A small sign over the bar announces that no aliens are allowed. Very promising. Will you approach one of the barmaids for a tip about who in the bar might best be approached for a bit of underworld 'largesse' (turn to 30), or just mingle to see what you can find out (turn to 362)?

300

The two cars fly over the crest, yours becoming slightly airborne. In front, the road turns into a tight curve. Neither of you has an atom's worth of hope of slowing in time to take it. The sloop brakes wildly; you crash into it from behind, and destroy your vehicle. Both cars, still travelling at great speed, fly off the road and wrap themselves around separate trees.

Throw three dice and deduct the total from your STAMINA. If you have survived the smash, turn to 359.

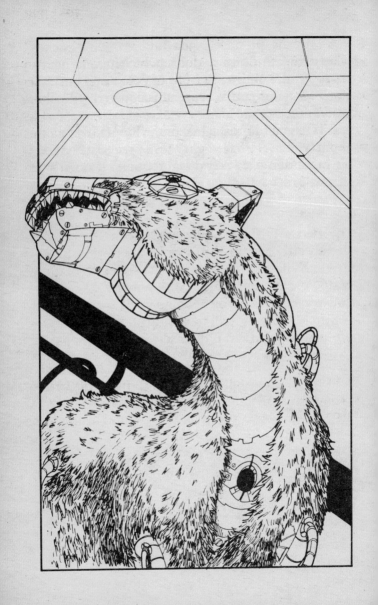

301

The ramp ends in a door, which opens as you approach. Standing in front of you is an enormous four-legged dog-like beast. It is covered with short spiky fur, but one of its eyes is a vidicamera and its teeth are stainless-steel razors. A low growl vibrates from its throat. Will you try to soothe it (turn to **223**) or just assume it's *very* dangerous and shoot it (turn to **262**)?

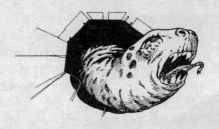

302

It darts towards you as you fly by. A great flash of electricity grazes past, burning through the back of your pressure-suit. Deduct 2 points from your STAMINA. However, you make it past, and head for the exit. Turn to **185**.

303

A bright flash of electrons surges out of the button, engulfing your arm. The door does not open. Lose 1 point of STAMINA. Return to **186**.

304

'Mind if I join in?' you ask, pulling a chair up to the circle of card players. 'Yeah, I do. Get lost,' says the woman. After a bit of wheedling, however, she changes her mind and lets you sit in. You discover that her name is Zera Gross and that, ostensibly, she runs an import/export agency. Aha! You try a pointed joke to see what reaction the word 'drugs' might have on them: 'More exporting than importing, I'd wager, the nature of the drug business being what it is! Ha, ha!' you laugh. The sudden silence and stony faces around the table is a little disconcerting.

'OK, boys, time to teach the little worm a bit of respect.' The five or six men with whom you were playing cards rise to their feet and attack you. You are beaten, as they say, almost to a pulp. Lose 2 STAMINA points permanently.

When you finally come to, the bar is almost empty. It is early morning. On the new day, after a bit of medical attention and rest, you head off to the City Central Library. There might be some information about Zera Gross on the case lists. Turn to **80**.

305

You grab the rafter and swing a kick at the first thug, sending him flying off the gantry to the floor far below. *Thud.* The other gunman slips his blaster off safety, but you have already closed with him. A kick sends the gun out of his hand and a few well-placed blows finish him off.

'Psst!' says someone back down the gantry. 'Psst, buddy!' It is a man, possibly one of Blaster's gunmen, crouching low, waving at you to come over. Will you follow him (turn to **227**), or run from him (turn to **266**)?

306

All of the hangars but one are deserted. In this one, you find a lone shuttle pilot performing systems checks on his spacecraft. He ignores you as he goes laboriously through panel after panel of instruments – flicking switches, reading meters, making adjustments. You decide to approach him for some information. Will you offer him cash for this information (turn to 267), or not (turn to 228)?

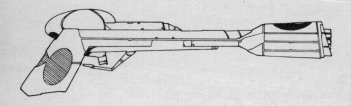

307

As you draw your pistol, the Grand Keeper murmurs a few words and makes a slight gesture across his lips with a finger. You discover you are frozen, incapable of movement. 'Now, let's be reasonable, shall we?' he says. 'Come, sir, sit down.' Turn to 268.

308

Will you secrete yourself away in the passenger arrivals section (turn to **269**) or in the freight depot (turn to **211**)?

309

The sports car flies over the crest, becoming momentarily airborne. In front of you, the road takes a sharp hairpin curve to the right. Very tricky. You slam on your brakes when you touch the ground and try to keep your car under control as it bucks into the bend. *Test your Luck*. If you are successful, turn to **251**; otherwise turn to **270**.

310

The car's turbines whine softly as you eke out the extra revs necessary to bring you alongside the criminals' car. You do so, slowly.

Will you try to shoot at them (turn to **291**), or push them off the raised road with a side-swipe (turn to **252**)?

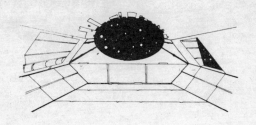

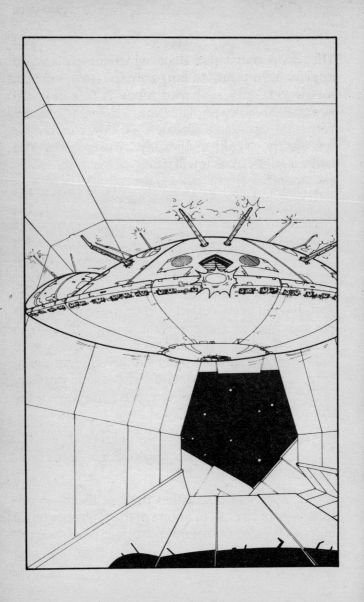

311

The ramp ends in a door which opens as you approach. In front is a long corridor occupied by a metre-wide, saucer-shaped robot. A flickering red eye on its rim contemplates you; a cluster of blasters set in its underside threaten. It hangs in the air noiselessly. 'Word of the day?' it demands. You make a guess. Which will it be:

Tuesday?	Turn to **155**
Satophil?	Turn to **194**
Wrench?	Turn to **272**
Babbet?	Turn to **233**

312

The asteroid is covered with batteries of phasers and, having been alerted to your presence by your passage through the minefield, is using them in an attempt to deprive you of your life. You will have to fight these outer defences before attempting to land. If you have any Smart Missiles left, you may launch them. For each Smart Missile deployed, the asteroid will lose 2 SHIELDS.

	WEAPONS STRENGTH	SHIELDS
ASTEROID DEFENCES	9	6

If you win, you may either dock at the main entrance (turn to **117**), or at one of the few emergency airlocks set into the asteroid's surface (turn to **273**).

313

The door opens into an identically cubic room. Turn to **186**.

314

The man does not look at all surprised when you join him. In fact, there seems to be a certain recognition in his eyes. You talk to him for a while about how you're an off-world travelling salesman, before mentioning that you'd be interested in 'expanding' your operations to cover, perhaps, a few 'illicit' items. He laughs at you. 'You're not a salesman. Ha! You're a narc.' This, of course, startles you slightly. He is quick to reassure you. Leaning closer, he whispers, 'We can't talk here. Meet me in two hours at the Hotel Mirimar, room 1201.' He then drains his glass, rises and walks from the canteen. You decide to meet him. Turn to **395**.

315

The Café Heroes of the Federation, you find, is a small establishment on the outskirts of the city. At 9.00 a.m. it is completely deserted. Seating yourself in a discreet position, you order breakfast and wait for Clive Torus. After two hours, the only other people who have been in the café are two old ladies who had a slice of toast between them, a young couple and a child. None of them could possibly have been Clive – looks like he's not going to show. Something may have happened to him, so you decide to follow him up. Will you ask the café owner if he's seen or heard from him (turn to **81**), or try to find his address (turn to **276**)?

316

Out the back is a large black ground car with reflective windows. They bundle you into the rear, keeping their guns trained on you. 'Time for a little ride – har, har,' laughs the driver. You are taken for a drive out of the city and into the country, to a large manor-house. There are shady-looking gunmen all over the grounds. As you are led out of the car, towards the house, you see an opportunity to escape – a quick dive into a privet hedge followed by a short roll down an embankment and then a sprint for all you're worth. Will you attempt this escape (turn to **277**), or let the gunmen lead you into the house (turn to **170**)?

317

It flaps its great wings to stand upright and considers you with unnerving malice. 'I am a Mind Parasite. One of the great old ones from ancient Kyth,' it says, in a voice of ice. Turn to **200**.

318

'Here,' you say, slipping him a wad of banknotes. 'This is for a cup of coffee. Isn't it coffee break now?' How many kopecks did you give him:

1,000?	Turn to 279
1,500?	Turn to 240
2,000?	Turn to 201

319

The car slides a bit, but your deftness keeps it on the road. You hurtle out of the bends at over 170 k.p.h., to find that the distance between your foes and yourself has been drastically shortened. They are now only about 100 metres in front. Turn to 154.

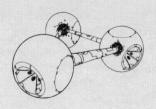

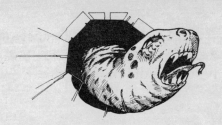

320

You hire a helijet and land among the other helijets on the pad on top of the fifty-storey Isosceles Tower. On the fiftieth floor you find the office you want: Z. GROSS AND ASSOCIATES. IMPORT/EXPORT.

Surprisingly, the door to this office is unlocked; in fact, ajar. You draw your blaster and slowly push the door open with a toe – you are faced by the wood-panelled wall of a corridor leading to the left and right. There is no sound whatsoever. Will you follow the wall to the left (turn to 331), or the right (turn to 86)?

321

You fire at each other!

ZERA   SKILL 8   STAMINA 11

If you defeat her, turn to 165.

322

You go off target and hit a couple of tentacles from a pair of the bulbous creatures. They open tremendous tooth-filled maws and attack you wildly, biting you. Lose 4 points of STAMINA. Turn to 244.

323

You part with your 500. The barmaid pulls you close and points out two people at separate tables. One is a pale, drawn-looking man alone with his beer, the other is a fat, middle-aged woman playing cards with six or seven men. Which will you approach, the man (turn to 314), or the woman (turn to 343)?

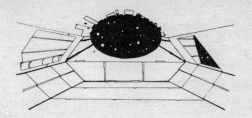

324

The manufacturing yearbooks are long, tedious and, what's worse, completely useless. They don't seem to contain anything remotely informative. After a few hours, you decide to try something different. If you haven't already, you can look up statistics on agriculture (turn to 363) or transport (turn to 285). If you're sick of statistics, you could look through old vidinews for references to organized crime (turn to 41).

325

Peering around a corner, you can see the gunman getting into a long black ground car, which then drives off. You hail the helicab and follow the saloon to a place called Spark's Bar. Here, the gunman gets out of the car, with the driver, and enters the bar. Turn to 286.

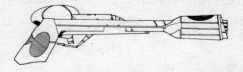

326

'. . . Yeah, Clive's wife is planning on meeting this Federal Investigator tomorrow morning . . .' you hear.

'What? With the documents?'

'Yeah – at the greenhouse in the Botanic Gardens.'

'The Fed doesn't know about it yet?'

'Nah . . . the boys are bringing the dude here for the set-up. I rang Clive's wife, posing as the Investigator, to get her to come . . .'

A door in the other room opens and a frightened voice cries, 'The Fed's escaped!'

'What?' They run from the room.

Will you go to this set-up meeting tomorrow (turn to 44), or just escape from the manor and look for some other clues (turn to 231)?

327

A short search reveals two very suspicious items: a man in a tree with a high-powered hunting blaster; and a long black ground sloop with darkened windows parked behind one of the greenhouses. You can't do much about the car, so will you take out the sniper (turn to 288), or assume he's harmless and just go to meet Mrs Torus anyway (turn to 376)?

328

You accelerate towards Rispin's End at a steady 3 Gs. When you arrive, will you survey the moon from orbit (turn to **289**), or land at the only base and take a closer look (turn to **250**)?

329

The forest ends, and the road, occupied only by the sloop 100 metres ahead, leads from it in a long graceful curve to the right. You could probably gain a bit on them by driving up the wrong side of the road, keeping an eye out for oncoming traffic, of course. Will you do this (turn to **37**), or not (turn to **290**)?

330

You hire a long-range helijet and fly out to the tiny, vegetation-covered island. As you circle over it, you spot a large clearing containing a launch pad for shuttles, two landing bays for helijets and an anti-grav dray. One of the helijet bays is occupied. You land your aircraft in the other bay and climb out. Now that you are closer, you can see three ramps, spaced equally around the helijet bays, descending into the ground. Two of the ramps end in quite ordinary-looking entrances, while the third finishes in a large freight door. Will you enter one of the ordinary entrances (turn to **311** or **301**), the freight door (turn to **67**), or take a look at the antigrav dray (turn to **281**)?

331

The corridor opens out into a spacious open-plan office. There are some fifteen desks spread about, computer vidilinks and even a few document files. It gives the impression of having been very hastily stripped and deserted. Files are spilled on the floor, magnetic memory tape lies everywhere, and one of the desks is even tipped on its side. Perhaps they were expecting a whole bevy of Feds to arrive. Will you search through some of the files to see if any sense can be made of this mess (turn to **242**), or will you continue through the office (turn to **203**)?

332

The passage leads to a room stacked high with heavy-duty plastic containers. Looking them over, you find they contain different chemicals, natural products and packaging materials – all the necessary raw materials to produce Satophil-d. You return to the crossways. If you haven't already done so, you may take either the right passage (turn to 146), or the continuation of the tunnel (turn to 293).

333

You land at Kether's only starport, which is on the continental land-mass and only ten kilometres from the planet's capital city. Your ship is towed to its parking-space where, to your dismay, you are boarded by several Customs officers looking for contraband. 'What, drugs?' you ask. They look at you smugly before replying. 'No, technology. And this,' says one of them, finding your spy ray, 'is an example of it. I'm sorry, this device is a prohibited import and as such will not be returned to you. Good-day.' They leave the spacecraft. Cross the spy ray off your Equipment List. Rather brusque treatment, and they didn't even check your cargo . . .

You could ask a few questions around the starport (turn to 394), go to the local law-enforcement headquarters and ask for some help (turn to 255), or, if you want to keep a really low profile, find a shady starport canteen in which to conduct a few discreet inquiries (turn to 299).

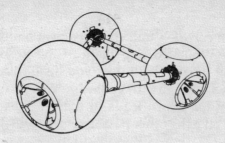

334

Your continued search reveals even more missing files, this time regarding spacecraft: whole interstellar flights are missing. Something is odd there. You leave the Computer Centre. Will you go and see the Air-traffic Chief about these missing records (turn to **89**), or try to find somebody in the space industry who may know something about any illegal space traffic (turn to **384**)?

335

He swears that he has told you the truth. It doesn't give you a great deal to go on, however: the best course of action seems to be to find someone in the space industry who can verify the existence of this illegal traffic. Turn to **384**.

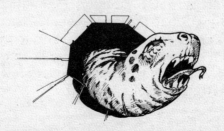

336

The dim corridor arches and ends at a rocky intersection. While floating there in the yellow light, deciding which way to go, you hear voices. Low, sonorous tones drift to your ears. Will you go down the corridor which leads to these voices (turn to 397), or take the other passage (turn to 385)?

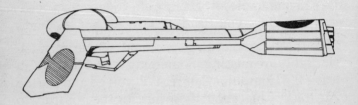

337

Time to decide your strategy regarding the Customs officials. You could approach a Customs officer and either threaten him for information (turn to 142), or, if you are willing to spend at least 2,000 kopecks, you could try bribery (turn to 298). Alternatively, you could hide in the Customs building in the hope of catching them in an illegal act (turn to 308).

338

You back your ship off, aim your phasers and blow the satellite to pieces. Having effectively destroyed your last clue, you head back to Kether starport. Turn to **16**.

339

As the black sloop reaches the crest, you spot a road to the right. There must be a curve up ahead! You slam on the brakes and slide to a halt just over the hill. In front, the road takes a tight turn. The black sloop, unable to slow in time to negotiate the curve with safety, has flown off the road and wrapped itself around a stout-looking tree. Turn to **359**.

340

The corridor leads to an automatic door, which sighs open as you approach and clangs shut after you go through. You are in another corridor. On one side, this corridor ends in a door, on the other it continues until it disappears around a corner. Will you go through the door (turn to **67**), or down the passageway (turn to **253**)?

341

You dive past it and head towards the exit. Turn to **185**.

342

An X-ray laser flashes on momentarily, burning your arm. The door does not open. Lose 1 point of STAMINA. Return to **186**.

343

The woman is really horrible – gap-toothed, beery, burping and coarse, but the way she commands the men playing cards with her shows that she has real power. What form of power, however, is yet to be seen. Will you try to join the card players (turn to **304**), or wait until they finish and then follow the woman (turn to **265**)?

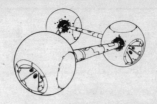

344

You grab the rafter and aim a kick at the first thug, but miss him. They overpower you with a few quick blows and then drag you along the gantry. Turn to **61**.

345

The starport is divided, roughly, into two sections: there are the enormous spaceship hangars, of which only one seems to be in use, and there are the administrative and traffic-control buildings. In which section will you begin inquiries? The hangars (turn to **306**), or the administrative block (turn to **150**)?

346

You follow the corridor for a few more minutes until your path is blocked by an iris lock, over which is inscribed: GRAND KEEPER. The lock opens as you approach and reveals a small room decorated in the most archaic taste. Evidently there is a gravity generator in the room, as an aged man in voluminous black robes is seated in a high-backed chair, facing you. 'Come in, come in,' he says, motioning you towards a stool at his feet. 'Come and sit for a while.' Will you do as he says (turn to 263), or assume he is hostile and draw your pistol (turn to 307)?

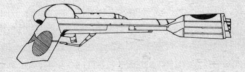

347

'Wait!' he cries, eyes flying open. 'I just remembered! The dope dealers' nerve-centre is in the city . . . er . . . wait . . . wait . . . let me see,' he pinches his brow with a couple of fingers as if trying to recall. 'Yes, I've got it, in the Isosceles Tower – top floor.' 'Thanks,' you say, as you tie him up with his vidiphone cord. You head into the city centre, towards the Isosceles Tower. Turn to **320**.

348

The sloop accelerates into the straight and disappears over a hill. It is still about 300 metres from your car. The hill it went over is a hump-backed ridge, so you cannot see how the rest of the road continues. As you approach the hill, will you assume that the road continues straight, and go over the crest at high speed (turn to **309**), or will you anticipate a corner and slow down a bit (turn to **163**)?

349
A shudder runs through your car and it begins to fishtail slightly across the road. The black car pulls away from you as you fight to maintain control. Turn to **290**.

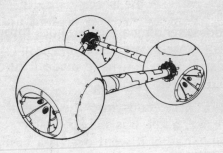

350
The man has no identification on him, no vendetta marks or anything, in fact, which could give you information. You can only determine the cause of death – loss of blood. In one of his hands, however, he holds 4 Pep Pills. You may add these to your Equipment List. You leave the room. Turn to **389**.

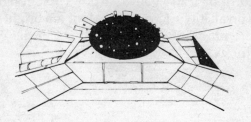

351

You misjudge the distance between your ship and a mine. The device's mass detectors are disturbed by the proximity and send a short message to the hydrogen bomb contained somewhere in its shell to explode.

This it does, sending a terrific shock through your spacecraft. Lose 2 SHIELDS. If this hasn't destroyed your vessel, then you have made it through the minefield. Turn to **312**.

352

The corridor leads you to a tiny cubic room with doors on all its surfaces. Each door is a bright shade of red with a little black button set in the centre. Turn to **225**.

353

You approach the dome which, you notice, is an oxygen tent. Around it are parked various low-gravity earth-moving machines and a rocket scooter. Looks like you're not going to suffocate after all. You knock on the airlock. After a few moments it flashes up a little sign: ENTER. Inside, you meet the owner, a wizened old prospector. He expresses some surprise when you tell him of your circumstances. 'Shot down, eh? Shot down by drug runners, you say? Well, shot down, maybe, but I don't know 'bout them drug runners. Been on this rock for thirty years, and ain't never come 'cross any of them ol' drug runners.' He feeds you, replenishes your oxygen tanks and then, with the new day, takes you on his rocket scooter to the dome town. Turn to **275**.

354

You follow after Clive, finding yourself in the cavernous main interior of the warehouse. In the dim light, you can see lots of crates and a large, sleek black ground car. Creeping forward, you are surprised by half a dozen gunmen leaping out from behind the crates. 'Freeze!' one of them yells. Will you do as he says (turn to **100**), or try to make a break for it (turn to **139**)?

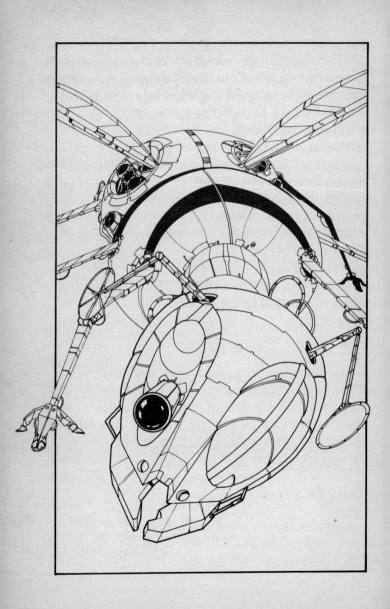

355

Deduct the 500 kopecks from your credit account. The miner informs you that a certain large asteroid known as C230 is the centre of a hive of activity – none of which is reported to the authorities. After receiving this news, you notice a small insect land on the table in front of you. Insect? No – a bug. An electronic bug, cunningly formed so as to look like a real insect; you can see the tiny jets under the mock wings and the vidicamera for an eye – looking straight into your own. Will you go to asteroid C230 (turn to **73**), or will you attempt to lose the bug (turn to **53**)?

356

Choose carefully! What question will you ask?

What type of beast is it?	Turn to **317**
What place have you stumbled upon?	Turn to **278**
What help can the beast give you?	Turn to **239**

357

You hide away in the locker you used previously. Turn to **45**.

358

The shoulders are soft and begin to collapse under the forces your vehicle is exerting on them. Roll two dice. If the result is higher than or equal to your SKILL, turn to **270**. If the result is less than your SKILL, turn to **319**.

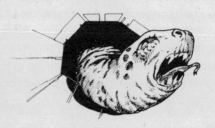

359

Leaving your own vehicle, you approach the wrecked sloop. Looking inside you can see that nobody survived. You recover the safety-deposit box and open it. Inside are lots of incriminating documents regarding two individuals: Zera Gross and 'Blaster' Babbet. There are bills for the raw materials necessary to produce Satophil-d, amounts paid in bribes to various officials and, what's most important, the location of their receiving facility on Kether! Evidently, the drug arrives from space via shuttle at a little island some 4,000 kilometres off the shore of the main continental land-mass. It is stored there until sent to the starport on Kether for shipment out of system. The box even contains the exact co-ordinates of the island facility. Turn to **330**.

360

The corridor leads to a door. It has a brass plate attached to it: ZERA GROSS. The door opens as you approach and there, in a room, behind a large desk, dictating to a little robot secretary, she is – fat, gap-toothed and horrible. 'Yeah?' she says, not looking at you, obviously thinking you're one of her henchmen. 'Whad' yer want?'

'Yeah?' repeats the secretary, scribbling frantically, 'Whad' yer . . .'

'Shuddup, dummy,' she shrieks at it. 'I'm speaking ter . . .' She notices who you are, '. . . *him*.' She makes a dive for a blaster on top of the desk.

Will you engage her in a gun fight (turn to **321**) or in hand-to-hand combat (turn to **282**)?

361

You make it to the second sphere and jump for the next. Roll two dice. If the result is higher than or equal to your SKILL, turn to **322**. If the result is less than your SKILL, turn to **244**.

362

You mingle for a while before finding a likely person. Throw a die: if the result is 1, the person is a pale drawn-looking fellow, who is alone (turn to **314**); if 2, the person is a fat middle-aged woman playing cards at a table (turn to **343**); if in the range 3–6, turn to **382**.

363

The agriculture yearbooks prove to be weighty but rather uninformative reading. After a couple of hours of annual rainfall, bushels of wheat and so many tons of dead animals, you decide that agriculture is probably not what you are looking for. If you haven't already, you can look at statistics for manufacturing (turn to 324) or transport (turn to 285). If you're sick of statistics, you could go and look through old vidinews for references to organized crime (turn to 41).

364

You dive down an alley and run. The gunman fires after you but misses and yells out, just before you round the next corner: 'You can't escape – not even in space!' What does he mean by 'not even in space'? You could try to find somebody in the space industry to talk to about illegal goings on out there (turn to 384), or you could double back to the café and try to follow the gunman (turn to 325).

365

The room has a corridor leading from it, and a door. Behind the door you can hear muffled voices. Will you try to hear what is being said (turn to 326), or explore down the corridor (turn to 287)?

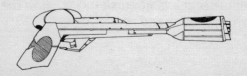

366

You look among a few copses of trees, under a shrub or two and in one of the greenhouses, but find nothing and nobody of a suspicious nature. You go to meet Mrs Torus. Turn to 376.

367

The asteroid belt lies some 4 AUs out in a huge ring around Aleph Cygni. It consists of at least a hundred thousand fair-sized rocks and millions of little ones. Once you reach the outskirts of a small section of the belt, you realize the futility of a search – it would take a Federal Astrosurvey team with ten ships a good twenty years to explore every rock capable of supporting a base. You head back to Kether. Turn to 333.

368

You follow the track at great speed, meet the main road, swing on to it and accelerate away. Turn to 56.

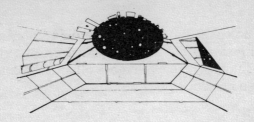

369
You're a bit slow, and the paperweight grazes your skull and knocks you out. You never regain consciousness. You have failed.

370
You make it through the minefield safely. The production asteroid is just a short way off. Turn to 312.

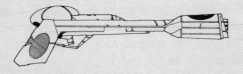

371
There's not much point in staying here, so you return to the crossways. If you haven't already done so, you may take either the left passage (turn to 332), or the continuation of the tunnel (turn to 293).

372

You accelerate towards the asteroid belt, your ship's twin fusion drive pushing you along at a steady 3 Gs. Suddenly, an alarm goes off and the command screen presents:

WARNING
  TWO UNIDENTIFIED VESSELS APPROACHING
  FROM ASTEROIDS ON INTERCEPT COURSE

You push your ship into a slight turn to avoid any possibility of a collision, but the two vessels, instead of continuing straight, change direction to remain on a collision course. They are trying to catch you. In fact, they have begun firing their phasers! You will have to fight them.

	WEAPONS STRENGTH	SHIELDS
INTERCEPTOR 1	5	3
INTERCEPTOR 2	5	2

If you destroy them, you may either continue towards the asteroids (turn to 367), or change course and go to Kether instead (turn to 333).

373

'Well, in that case . . .' he says, taking the money from your hands, 'I might let you sit at this terminal here for a few minutes.' He indicates a vidilink behind the reception counter. 'But you must be quick, as my superior could return at any moment and then . . . alas . . . I would have to denounce you.' He smiles. 'My neck or yours.' You sit at the terminal and begin looking through the Centre's confidential files. Turn to 393.

374

You throw him around the room a bit and then place the barrel of your blaster firmly against his forehead.

'Now,' you say. 'Tell me the truth.'

'It is, it is,' he screams. 'I swear it is. Look . . . look, I'll even tell you which asteroid all the traffic's been coming from.'

'OK.'

'It's C230 – if you've got a Cosmo-Nav you can't miss it.'

Will you go out to this asteroid (turn to 73), or try to find somebody in the space industry who might be able to verify this source of illegal traffic (turn to 384)?

375

The niche contains a small plaque:

PRAYER TO THUVALD
Hidden is he,
Mighty is he,
His time returns,
Hold, wait, be still.

Strange! Finding nothing else, you continue out of the room and down the still rough-hewn corridor. Turn to **336**.

376

You walk towards her. 'Mrs Torus,' you say. She turns, but at that moment two shots ring out from a copse of trees to your left – one slams into Mrs Torus, the other into you. Throw one die and deduct the result from your STAMINA. If you survive, continue.

You both fall to the ground, Mrs Torus dropping the bag she was carrying. The safety-deposit box with the incriminating documents falls out. Before you can react, the sniper dashes over, grabs the box and leaps into a sloop, which squeals off.

What a set-up! You lurch to your feet. Will you attempt to chase the sloop (turn to **191**), or aid Mrs Torus (turn to **210**)?

377

You manoeuvre your spacecraft alongside the satellite. It is very large, obviously containing a nuclear-power plant, instead of using a solar wing. An omni-directional receiver antenna sticks out of one end, and a unidirectional antenna points out of the other – down at Kether's capital city. Will you blow the satellite up (turn to **338**), or don your pressure-suit and take a space-walk across to look at it (turn to **399**)?

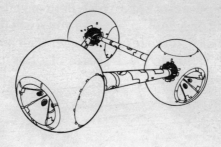

378

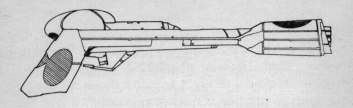

378

You tail-gate them up a straight at 240 k.p.h. Every now and then you graze their bumper with yours and push them slightly. The road climbs a hill and then disappears over the crest. Both of your cars are still doing over 200 k.p.h. when you reach the ridge. Roll two dice. If the result is higher than or equal to your SKILL, turn to **300**. If the result is less than your SKILL, turn to **339**.

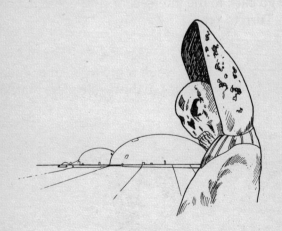

379

The passage leads to a room. In the centre, hanging in mid-air, is a large, square plastic table – the latest thing in antigravity furniture, evidently. A chair, similarly without legs, hovers next to it. When you enter the room this chair floats over and says, 'Hi! Want to sit on me?' Pathetic device. You see a key, with a large cardboard tag attached to it, lying on the chair. Picking it up, you read:

> *Zera,*
> *This is for shutting down the reactor at Base 1. Keep it safe.*
> *Blaster*

You pocket it. There's nothing else in the room, so you go back to the intersection and down the corridor. Turn to **340**.

380

Roll two dice. If the result is higher than or equal to your SKILL, turn to **224**. If the result is less than your SKILL, turn to **263**.

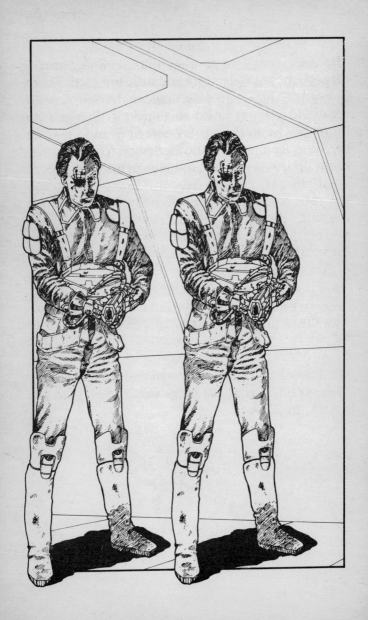

381

The door opens on to a sumptuous living-area – carpets, modern furniture and diffused light. There is even a trendy folding screen, decorated with off-world scenery, next to the door. In the wall opposite the door you are standing in is a wide corridor, leading into another, similarly decorated room. In this corridor stand two identical figures of what must be 'Blaster' Babbet. Tucked under each left arm is an enormous Vanque blaster. 'Good evening,' they say together. 'Time to die, Fed.' Will you blast the left figure (turn to **69**), the right figure (turn to **108**), or try to think of an alternative course of action (turn to **147**)?

382

You find a slightly deranged starship navigator to talk to. He grabs you by the neck as you stand at the bar and says in a low voice, 'Beware.' Well, he might know something. You buy him a drink and sit at a table with him. Turn to **245**.

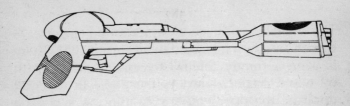

383

The rafter is above you! You jump for it. *Test your Luck*. If you are successful, turn to **305**; otherwise turn to **344**.

384

Will you conduct your inquiries at Kether's starport (turn to **345**), or in the city (turn to **131**)?

385

The passage winds through the rocks, eventually leading past a large dark room occupied solely by a low pedestal upon which a ruddy flame is burning. The entrance to the chamber is flanked by two large, iron-studded wooden doors. Will you enter the room (turn to **83**), or bypass it (turn to **346**)?

386

'That's all I know!' he pleads. Looks like you're not going to make much headway here, so you decide to go and look for the satellite that he mentioned. Turn to **36**.

387

The sloop is about 300 metres ahead, clocking 165 k.p.h. It is tearing around a long, wide, left curve, towards a straight. A small access road is coming up on your left. If you take it you may be able to cut the distance between the two vehicles – but there is a danger that the access road might not join up with the main road further on. If you decide to take the side-road, turn to 241. If you stay on the main road, turn to 348.

388

You maintain a steady distance between the vehicles. Turn to 37.

389

You exit the room into a corridor. Turn to 253.

390

The airlock proves safe to hold. After a few moments the iris lock clicks shut and air roars back into the room. Turn to 371.

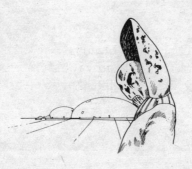

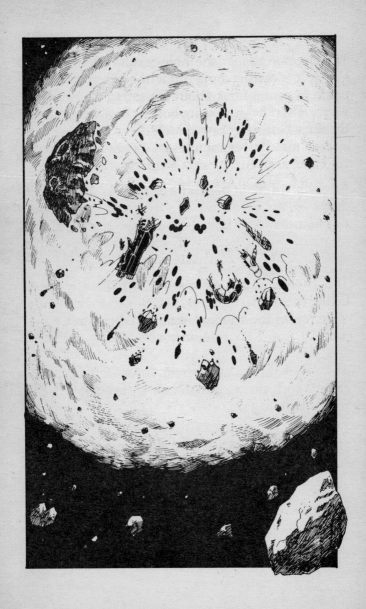

391

Turning the key in the hole results in a horrible grinding noise coming from the reactor. Sirens begin to sound throughout the asteroid's passageways. A synthesized voice booms: 'Warning. Gravity shielding withdrawn. Melt-down will occur in approximately five minutes . . . Warning. Gravity . . .' and so on.

All the instrument panels flash in panic. The ceiling drops away to reveal a small airlock, marked EMERGENCY EXIT. It leads you to the surface of the asteroid. From here you scuttle back to your spacecraft and make a hasty retreat.

The asteroid explodes in a ball of radioactive fire, taking the refinery, stores, shuttles and – evidently – the rest of the criminal organization with it. Congratulations. Your mission is a success.

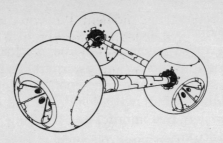

392

You begin to run towards the ridge in front of you; you are virtually flying in the low gravity. After half an hour you cross it, only to be confronted with more of this seemingly endless moon, grey plains and splintered mountains rolling on to the horizon. A red warning light – ten minutes of oxygen – has just come on inside your helmet. You try to run back to the orange dome you saw earlier, but somewhere along the way your oxygen is finally depleted. You have failed.

393

Consulting the file directory on the terminal reveals that you can only have access to transport files – nothing personal, legal or even remotely criminal. So you have a quick look through the transport files and notice, almost immediately, that large sections are missing from the air-traffic records – days, weeks, maybe more. There has either been some enormous bureaucratic incompetence or, as seems more and more likely, a cover-up. What could they be hiding? Flights from certain locations? You could be discovered at any moment. Will you continue to search through the files (turn to 334), or go in search of the person most likely to be responsible for the missing files, the Chief of Air-traffic Control (turn to 89)?

394

The starport is a large place, but there are few people about; the only other craft present are a small non-hyperspace fighter and a squat planet-to-orbit shuttle. You manage to find a few people to chat to about Kether's starport, although all you find out is that it is the only facility in the system which can handle the refuelling of starships. If this is true, then it means that all the drugs that are leaving Aleph Cygni must pass through this starport. Well, maybe. Not finding any more interesting topics of conversation you decide to leave the starport's environs. Will you declare your Federal Investigator status to the local law-enforcement headquarters to see what information they have (turn to 255), or find a starport canteen, or hotel, in which to conduct your investigations (turn to 299)?

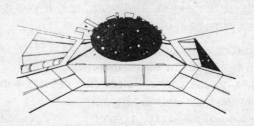

395

It is night. The Hotel Mirimar is a dive. The elevator is out of order. There is no heating. Arriving at the twelfth floor after running up the stairs, you lean for a moment in the doorway to catch your breath. The door to 1201, which is just next to you, opens. A shifty-looking character, putting something in his jacket pocket, steps out. He looks a bit surprised at seeing you. He waits impatiently by the elevator until, realizing that it is out of order, he heads for the stairs, and clatters off down towards street level. Will you enter 1201 (turn to 236), or follow the man who just left (turn to 295)?

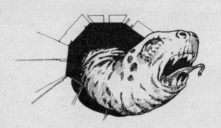

396

At a touch of the accelerator, your car leaps at the massive black sloop. *Test your Luck*. If you are successful, turn to 8; otherwise turn to 57.

397

Cautiously, you drift towards the voices, until you come to a room. The passage seems to enter it through the ceiling, for there, upside down in the zero gravity, two figures are floating. They are each garbed head to toe in large sack-like black robes. They look like some order of weightless monks.

'The holy malevolence is stirring again,' says one.

'Yes,' says the other. 'It is.'

'It will be wanting a . . . toy again,' continues the first.

'Yes, it will.'

Will you stay where you are (turn to **258**), confront them (turn to **63**), or retreat back to the intersection and down the other passage (turn to **385**)?

398

You rocket out to Rispin's End for a look. It is a tiny, almost asteroid-sized lump of rock, hardly more than 400 kilometres in diameter. There is only one official facility on this moon – a small dome town for scientists and tourists. The population is about 300 persons. Will you land at this facility (turn to **275**), or fly around the moon to see if anything unusual can be spotted (turn to **50**)?

399

You will have to use hand-held zero-gravity jets to bridge the gap between yourself and the satellite. These contain limited fuel, so every time you make a decision (that is, turn to a new reference), make a mark on a scrap of paper with your pen. Once you have 4 marks, you are out of fuel and spin off into space. Stop making marks if you reach the satellite. You steady yourself in the open iris of your airlock and take careful aim with your jets at the satellite. Roll two dice. If the result is higher than or equal to your SKILL, turn to **65**. If the result is less than your SKILL, turn to **260**.

Don't forget to keep count of your fuel.

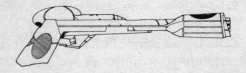

400

With the capture of 'Blaster' Babbet you have wiped out the leadership of the criminal organization. Congratulations – you have smashed the drug ring. Your mission is a complete success.

Another Adventure Gamebook

MAELSTROM

Alexander Scott

Imagine a band of travellers on the long road from St Albans to London – a dangerous journey in troubled times. Which will YOU be – an alchemist, skilled in the dark arts of magic, a rogue on the run from justice, a noble lady on her way to stir up intrigue at court, a spy disguised as a herbalist carrying vital messages to the King, or any one of a host of different characters . . .

YOU choose the characters, YOU decide the missions and YOU have the adventures in the turbulent world of Europe in the sixteenth century – either as a player or as the referee.

Complete with Beginners' and Advanced Rules, Referee's Notes, maps, charts and a solo adventure to get you started, *Maelstrom* is a great game for three or more players.

Steve Jackson's

SORCERY! 1

THE SHAMUTANTI HILLS

Your search for the legendary Crown of Kings takes you to the Shamutanti Hills. Alive with evil creatures, lawless wanderers and bloodthirsty monsters, the land is riddled with tricks and traps waiting for the unwary traveller. Will you be able to cross the hills safely and proceed to the second part of the adventure – or will you perish in the attempt?

SORCERY! 2

KHARÉ – CITYPORT OF TRAPS

As a warrior relying on force of arms, or a wizard trained in magic, you must brave the terror of a city built to trap the unwary. You will need all your wits about you to survive the unimaginable horrors ahead and to make sense of the clues which may lead to your success – or to your doom!

SORCERY! 3

THE SEVEN SERPENTS

Seven deadly and magical serpents speed ahead of you to warn the evil Archmage of your coming. Will you be able to catch them before they get there?

SORCERY! 4

THE CROWN OF KINGS

At the end of your long trek, you face the unknown terrors of the Mampang Fortress. Hidden inside the keep is the Crown of Kings – the ultimate goal of the *Sorcery!* epic. But beware! For if you have not defeated the Seven Serpents, your arrival has been anticipated . . .

> Complete with all the magical spells you will need, each book can be played either on its own, or as part of the whole epic.

STARLIGHT ADVENTURE 1:
STAR RIDER
Carole Carreck

For the first time in your life, you are the proud owner of a beautiful mare, Braid, and you know that the pair of you could reach the top, given half a chance. But competition is fierce in the professional world of horses. The stakes are high, the risks are real, and it soon becomes clear that some people are prepared to play very dangerously indeed. Who will you trust? The rich owner, Charles Bingham? The mysterious Andre Yates? Or will you try to go it alone?

STARLIGHT ADVENTURE 2:
THE RIDDLE OF THE RUNAWAY
Heather Fisher

YOU are a young detective, newly recruited to an important detective agency. Your first mission is to track down the irresistible heir to a fortune, who has run off with a rock band on tour in America. How will YOU cope, caught up in the high-powered world of record agents, casinos and pop parties?

available Spring 1985

STARLIGHT ADVENTURE 3:
ISLAND OF SECRETS
Kim Jordan

Somewhere on the sun-drenched island of Simnos, the legendary treasure of Aphrodite lies hidden. Or so you hear when you arrive there to begin your exciting new job as a villa girl. Almost unwittingly, you are swept up into a thrilling treasure hunt, only to discover that someone else is searching for the gold too – someone who is prepared to be utterly unscrupulous. Could it be the gorgeous windsurfer? Could it be the mysterious Englishman? Or could it be someone infinitely more dangerous.

STARLIGHT ADVENTURE 4:
DANGER ON THE AIR
Elizabeth Steel

Something is going sour at Radio South. The bustling, lively atmosphere of this thriving local radio station, where YOU are a reporter, has taken a turn for the worse. There's a hint of scandal in the air – a scandal that could spell disaster for the station and everyone involved. It is up to YOU to find out who's behind it.

Could it be Gerry Smith, streetwise, always with an eye to the main chance? Could it be Ron, the brash and unpredictable lead singer of the Bandits? Or could it be someone far more sinister?